I0520004

A Perfect Passion

By Piper Kay

2

Published by **Hot Ink Press**

An Erotic Imprint of

Crushing Hearts and Black Butterfly Publishing

This Book is sold subject to the condition that it shall not, by way of trade or otherwise, be lent, re-sold, duplicated, hired out, or otherwise circulated without the publisher's prior written consent in any form of binding or cover other than that in which it is published and without similar condition including this condition being imposed on the subsequent purchaser.

Thanks to the girls in my writers group for all the love and support. I honestly have no idea what I would do without you. A special thanks to Michelle Carnes, Monique Lomino, Nikki Prince, and Kim Carmichael. This story would not be seeing the light of day without your support and guidance. And to one special lady, SJ Davis, thanks so much for believing in me. I'll never be able to thank you enough.

Chapter One

After jotting down all the guy's hours, I pull off my hard hat, and get in my truck. I'm leaving work early, so I can get home to Aaron. It's our second month anniversary and I want to surprise him. Things have been moving along quickly, but it all seems to be working out half way decent. Well, except the part of Aaron being able to barely hold on to his business. He's got a construction company, but the competition is fierce, he hasn't been getting to many contracts lately in this economy, but he's a fighter and will come out on top, he always does. It's one of the things that drew me to him.

Aaron and I met at a party via a mutual friend. The attraction was immediate. He's a very handsome man, tall like I love, with long sexy legs, a great sense of humor, and a kind heart. One thing led to another and BAM, here we are living together.

When I bought this house, I did it on the cool. Aaron and I hadn't talked about living together, but every night one of us was staying at the others place, so this seemed like the logical next step. I had my old house up for sale prior to us meeting, because I needed to be closer to work in downtown Houston. Thing worked out just like a jigsaw puzzle, everything fell into place for us.

I'd called a local realtor friend and she showed me several houses. This one was perfect. It's a two-story brick Italian style home with four bedrooms, three baths, a gourmet kitchen, grand formals, custom faux painting and plaster moldings. The master bath comes with his and her separate rooms, custom closets, Lutron lighting, copper gutters, with an incredible pool and spa. It even has a little fountain. It's a beauty for sure and cost me a pretty penny. I didn't mind though, I fell in love at first sight.

Aaron and I had a blast shopping for the furniture. We chose modern leather black and white matching curved sofas, with glass tabletops in the middle and the end tables are topped with European deco lamps. Two leather recliners sit on both sides of the fireplace. Our bedroom is decorated with a Nora contemporary set with an illuminated frost headboard and a matching bench. We made sure to deck out the place with some scattered modern handmade abstract paintings.

I stroll through the front door tossing my keys in the basket. Aaron isn't downstairs anywhere, maybe he's outside in the pool or sunbathing, he loves it out there.

I pour a drink and exit through the French doors that open to the backyard. I spot Dax, our pool man. He's a bit hard to miss, the man is a six foot seven inch, blond, fuck-hot freaking Adonis. He's here doing the weekly clean. *If he weren't straight, I would sell my soul for a taste of that.*

"Hey there Dax, working hard?"

"Hi Damien, you know it. How are things going in the corporate world?"

"Great, just great." I wink, knowing it makes him nervous. "Have you seen Aaron? I thought maybe he was out here." *Dax is too fun to flirt with it makes him stutter.*

"No-nope. I haven't seen him. But, I used my own key for the gate, I didn-didn't knock on the door." Dax shields his eyes blocking out the setting sun. A pink flush creeps into his cheeks.

Dax is just too much! "Okay thanks. How're things going with you? How's Marcy?" I lean against the grill, hooking my thumbs in my pockets.

"Ugh, that's a long story. Things just didn't work out so well. We split last week." He shrugs his shoulders and his blond hair falls around his shoulders.

"Damn, really sorry to hear that man. Other fish in the sea and all that." *He really doesn't know how damn sexy he is. Makes him even hotter.*

"Yeah, I suppose so. Not really looking right now though. I figure it's better to stay single a while. I'm a bit burnt out on meaningless relationships anyway, that gets old quick." He flashes me a smile and continues cleaning the pool.

"I understand that. Well, I'm off to find Aaron. You have a good one." I wave to him as I turn and head back into the house.

"Same to you Damien."

Dax won't have a problem staying single with that long blonde hair that trails past his shoulders and cobalt blue eyes. I can guarantee that.

Back in the house, I speed up the spiral staircase towards the bedroom, still laughing inside about Dax. Aaron must be on the phone, I hear him mumbling and laughing. I love his laugh, it's so deep and raspy, but has a hint of kid-like innocence spun into it somehow.

I turn the brass doorknob and slowly open the door. I peek through the crack in the doorway and my heart skips a beat. *No way!*

My face heats with anger and shame. I shake my head from side to side in an attempt to clear my vision. My eyes are not deceiving me. A knot forms in the pit of my stomach. A cold sweat bead drips down my forehead and my pulse races. My breath puffs out in ragged gasps. *I might hyperventilate.*

Aaron's in our bed, he's naked with another man. I can't tell who he is; all I see is dark black hair. My heart's being stoned like a witch in Salem, and it feels like someone just played gladiator on my heart with a sledgehammer, pieces splinter inside my chest cavity.

My mouth won't cooperate with me. I can't get enough air to vibrate into my throat to even speak or yell. I gulp, like a guppy sucking air at the top of a dirty fish bowl.

I close my eyes, rub my lids, and look again. Aaron's scrunched up behind him, thrusting himself into the man. Faster and faster, he lets out a throaty moan as he pumps into him. His eyes are closed and he bites his lower lip. He's really into it and it makes me ill. He throws his head back, his long brown hair flips over his head, and falls to the middle of his back. He arches his entire body backwards, causing his pelvic region to push into the man. He glides in and out of him. *I'm going to hurl...*

"Fuck Aaron, oh God you feel good," the stranger in *our* bed purrs.

"You like this, huh? I'm gonna cum all over that sweet ass right now just like you want me to." He smacks the man's ass.

Aaron jabs several quick thrusts into him, letting out a loud groan, "Oh yes!"

I slap my hand up to my mouth, trying to cover it before I choke on my own saliva, but it's too late. Aaron hears me and turns my direction. Our eyes meet, mine full of disgust, his full of ecstasy, yet shock at the same time. I hate that the ecstasy part outweighed the shock.

"Fuck!" Aaron pulls out of the other man and reaches for a towel. "Damien, I'm...ah shit. I'm sorry, it's not what…"

Breathe! I'm sucking in air as hard as I can to find my voice. *Please let my lungs work now.*

"It's not what, Aaron? What it looks like?" I shake my head in detest.

"Please listen to me Damien."

The man scrambles in the sheets to cover himself and scans the room for his lost clothes. *They are strewn from the door to the bed dude, good luck getting them!* He looks from me to Aaron, not sure what's about to happen. Neither am I right now, but bat shit crazy on his bitch ass comes to mind.

I shake my head. "Get out, get the fuck out now!"

I try to make my way to the bathroom. I'm going to spew. I blast the cold water from the faucet in my face. Anger takes over me. Shock and rage is more like it. How dare he bring this dicklick into our home, into our bed for fuck's sake? The last few months were nothing but a lie? A fucking game to him, that didn't mean anything? I dry my face off gathering what little composure I can muster and walk out.

Aaron is sitting on the side of the bed. The mystery dick is gone, he must have rushed out half naked.

"Pack your stuff."

"Damien, can we please just talk?" Aaron makes his way towards me.

"Yes, allow me to do the talking.

14

Pack…your…stuff…and…get…the…hell…out…of…my…house!" I hold my hand out, stalling his approach on me.

"But Damien…" He holds his arms out like he wants to hug me.

"Goddammit, you don't hear well do you? I'm going outside. I'm going to give you half an hour. Pack what you need. I want your house key left in the basket, along with your copy of my truck key. And I want you gone."

I turn my back on him and head towards the bedroom door. I spin to face him when I reach the doorway glaring daggers. "Lose this number, as well as my cell, and work numbers too. As a matter of fact, forget my name while you're at it. We will not talk, nor discuss this, we won't try to work this out, and we will not give this time to pass. It's done and over with. Leave!" Practically swallowing my own tongue, I turn and leave the room. I'll start hurling insults if I don't. This is hard, very freaking hard, but I won't be made a fool of, not in my own house. This is the reason I don't do relationships, you can't trust people, not anyone. It stabs swords through your heart, and personally I don't like being hurt, nor stabbed for that matter. I don't do pain or emotions very well.

After pouring a glass of Bourbon, I swallow down a big gulp and escape the atmosphere inside the house to the fresh air outside. The air was so thick you could cut it with a knife. Dax is still here working, but I don't say a word. I flop down in the lawn chair, running my fingers through my hair, yanking it through the knot at the end.

I inhale deeply. I rub my hand over my forehead wiping the sweat off. My throat burns and my mind races a million miles a minute. I can't keep up with the spiraling emotional rollercoaster right now. Maybe I'm in shock, but the rage is building real quick.

I choke down the remainder of my Texan toxic and slam the glass down on the patio table next to me. Yep, that temper of mine just arrived. I plow through the phases of grief in about three minutes flat, denial and shock took a few minutes to get past, but anger jumps right in and takes over almost immediately. The bargaining stage won't come into play here, I don't bargain. I'll skip straight into acceptance after I'm past this anger. *I'm livid fucking mad.*

"Everything all right there, Damien?" Dax puts the pool net down, heading over in my direction.

"No Dax, it's so far from being okay right now, it's not even funny." I cup my hands over my face trying to wipes the horrid images away that are burned into my brain.

"Anything I can do?"

"No. Wait yes, would you mind stepping in the house and grabbing the bottle on top of the bar? I can't go in there right now and I need another drink, like yesterday."

"Um…yeah, no problem." A confused expression crosses Dax's face.

"Grab yourself a glass if you want one."

He nods and walks into the house, returning a minute later with the whiskey in one hand, and a glass in another. He pours himself a glass and hands me the bottle.

Without a word, Dax stares at me. I can only assume he's trying to figure out what the hell is going on right now. It's not like we're strangers, he's been my pool guy for a couple of years, from back in my old house and now here. We've talked plenty of times. He knows I was 'living as a couple' with Aaron, but I kind of doubt he's wanting to hear all the nitty-gritty details of what I just witnessed.

I tip the whiskey bottle straight up, and take a long pull off of it, then pass it back to him. I hear the French doors open, I know its Aaron. I'd told him we were done, there's nothing to talk about.

"Damien, can I have a word?" Aaron's voice waivers.

I never turn to look at him. "Aaron, you're about to see my goddamned temper. Get the fuck out of my house."

The French door slams causing the glass panes to rattle when he jerks it behind him. I hear the front door slam a few seconds later. The motor of his Mustang roars as he revs it up, but I don't hear him leave.

The side gate swings open smacking into the fence and Aaron saunters through it. "Dax, move your fucking truck so I can get the hell out of this place."

I stand to say something, but Dax gives me a wink. Aaron storms back out the gate.

"I got this Damien, nothing I can't handle. I'll be back in a few days to finish up." Dax gets out of the chair, setting the glass on the table.

"Thanks and sorry about this. It has nothing to do with you." I down the rest of my whiskey, savoring the burn in my throat.

"I know. Catch ya in a couple days. If you need anything call me." Dax grabs his things and struts out the gate, locking it behind him.

I have no worries, Aaron isn't stupid enough to start something with the bulked out pool guy. He'll be slaughtered like a lamb if he does.

Chapter Two

It's dark when I wake. I get to my feet, kicking the pebbles across the ceramic paver tiles that surround the entire pool decked area. The electric motor grinds from the shaft of the pump area, vibrating through the little hole in the exterior lid, bubbles pop out the escape hatch.

I go back into the house, remembering bits and pieces like a firefly that buzzes into the dome light ten times over. It's kind of blurry and unreal. I can't really find the lesson in this all, except that you never know everything about anyone. I've got a tornado of emotions and raw feelings twisting in my head.

My first step is to back track into the bedroom and remove the memories that have been engrained there over the last two months. The lingering scent of musty sex and remnants of disgust almost floor me. *I want to gag*! There are too many leftovers on the emotional railroad tracks. *Stop this mind fuck on yourself already Damien!*

I'm not usually one to dwell in sob stories or misery. I'm the type who brushes themselves off quickly and carries on with shit. It's how I've always been and how I'll be now. This is why I avoid emotional attachments. Denial is a great manipulator to someone who doesn't close it out on purpose. I do!

I halt bullshit dramatics on the spot. When it scrapes all of your insides, you instinctively hit the kill switch on all emotions and kick the fail-safe to feelings on the spot. It ends here!

I change all the sheets on the king sized bed. Yesterday this was our bed--our room—but today it's nothing but the shitty feeling of betrayal and no respect for anything that was ever important.

My phone rings, it's him of course. Aaron's cell number shows up but I ignore it. He doesn't leave a message. Ten minutes later, it's his brother's number. Did he think I would fall for that? *What a fucking cock-douche.* The third call comes from an unknown number. I let the machine pick it up. It's Aaron, of course, on a rampage. I'm actually amazed that he's finding a way to twist his fuck-up on me? Come on now, I wasn't the one in our bed banging the hell out of someone else.

The fourth, fifth, and still a sixth call come in. They're all from a mixture of unknown and private numbers. I blast Drowning Pools Thirty-Seven Stitches on the surround sound downstairs and grab another glass of whiskey. I don't want to hear the fucking phone or even glance to see the light on it revealing how many voicemails I have.

I don't know who I'm madder at, him or myself? I cared about Aaron, a lot. I'm not sure you'd call it head over heels in love, but it was enough for us to shack up together and give it a shot. Aaron could be a little on the bratty side, but it was kind of cute. He was almost needy at times, but to be honest, I liked the attention he gave me more than anything else. I liked being able to take care of him, but this--it's unforgivable.

Three more calls come in, holy fuck, does he ever give up? I downed the last sip of bourbon and slam the glass down, almost shattering the damn thing.

Snatching the receiver off the stand, I practically break the damn thing in my clenched fist.

"What the fuck Aaron? Goddamn you inconsiderate ass, do you not take a freaking hint? I have nothing to say to you. Nothing!"

"Damien?" the voice says. *Oops.*

"What? Who is this?"

"Oh-uh Damien, it's Dax from All Star Pool Cleaners."

"Oh Dax crap, I'm sorry man. I have your cell number programmed into my house contacts, but it didn't show up." Shit, the poor man will never want to work for me again.

"Well, I have an explanation for that. I'm calling from the hotel because I left my cell sitting outside on the deck at your house. It's on you're a/c unit."

"Oh all right, I'm sorry. What can I do for you, did you need me to get it and bring it in for you?"

"Would it be all right if I dropped by to get it?"

"Sure, whatever you need, that's fine Dax. I'll be up. Let me get Granger inside so he doesn't get all protective."

"Oh that dog is an old softie. I'll swing by in about twenty."

I hang up the phone. Not what I need tonight, but I don't want to be a total asshole about it either. It's just bad timing is all. I pull Granger my Rottweiler inside and he barrels up the stairs. He heads straight for my bed, where he sleeps every night. He's such a big baby. I follow him and change into shorts and a blue wife beater. Giving him a few pats on the head before going back downstairs, I turn off the light and walk down.

This time in Houston is perfect for keeping the doors and windows to be open, so I do just that. The temps at night are in the low eighties. I walk outside and light the tiki torches that surround the patio area. I'm going to do a few laps in the pool later.

I hear Dax's Suzuki Hayabusa when he makes the corner onto my street. It's one bad-ass bike, a black and red 2012 model. His keys jingle when he enters them into the lock on the side gate. My tunes crank back out after the quite track change.

I finish pouring my drink and light a smoke. Holding the cig in between my lips, I glance up. Long and muscular 'fuck me now' legs strut into view. Inhaling a puff, I keep watching. Black Afterburner boots, mid-calf, accentuate his tight, button-up jeans.

His cuff hangs on top of his boots, he reminds me of a longhaired, blond James Dean. Following the length of the jeans, my gaze skims upwards to his yellow wife beater. The ripples in his chest, fuck me sideways! Where did those come from? Normally he's in some kind of oversized T-shirt. His shirt matches his dirty-blond hair that's blowing freestyle in the wind, and waves across his right shoulder. The tats on his right arm intrigue me, the shape of tribal vintage, traipsing down, blending into his muscle structure almost stop my breath. *Fuckingshit!* I take the cigarette out of my mouth, and exhale a puff of smoke.

"Hi Dax." I lick my lips. I can't help it.

"Shit boss. You-ya kind of freak a guy out much? I'm sorry if I kept you up. You didn't need to stay up just because of my absentmindedness and being forgetful."

"I didn't. Just having a hard time getting to sleep, after everything that went on earlier, you know?" I give him a wicked grin.

"You do-doing all right? Heard from him?" He takes a deep breath.

"Nah, don't want too. My phone's been blowing up, but he crossed a line. I just can't backtrack over that kind of thing like nothing ever happened."

"Not trying to pry, but exactly what did happen with you and Aaron?" He sparks up a smoke.

"Well, the fucktwat decided to bring someone else into our home, into our bed."

"Ouch! Damn, I'm sorry Damien."

"Don't be, shit happens. My biggest problem is that sometimes I allow myself to trust, when no trust has been earned. Does that make any sense?"

"Perfectly! Know it all too well. That's the same problem I had with Marcy. You got a beer I can snag?"

"Beer, an assortment of whiskeys, toxins and mixed, etc…pick your poison."

"Cool, thanks. Don't mind if I do." He pours a glass of whiskey. "So are you okay or do you want to talk about it or anything?"

I can tell he doesn't want to talk about me and my ex-boyfriend, lover or whatever he's called now. I sidestep the convo, trying to remove the awkwardness.

"Yeah, I'm okay or I will be."

"So what happened with you and Marcy?"

"The same thing practically. I came in early from work and caught her half naked wrapped around some dudes waist. " He took a long swig from his glass.

"What is it with people? Damn, sorry."

"Wish I knew Damien. Needless to say, I kicked her to the curb, not technically but I left. I don't do sharing. The pissfuck can have her."

"My thoughts about Aaron too," I smile. "Need a refill?"

"Sure, why not. I don't have any plans for the night, just hanging out with myself. I thought about taking a ride around town on the ole' bike."

"Sounds like fun. I should break out my Harley Night-Rod special one night and cruise around myself."

"Yeah, I'd like to see you cruise on that bad-boy. Screw these mucky's in our lives, let's ride."

"Yeah, you really want to?" He nods. "You're right. I gotta change first Dax, give me a few."

"No problem, just going to enjoy the tunes while you get ready."

I take the steps two at a time on the way up to my room, and change into my leathers and stomp boots. I grab my jacket from the hall closet on the way downstairs.

"Nice stompers man."

"Thanks, my favorite kind. You ready?"

"Let's do it to it man." I head towards the kitchen and out though the door in the laundry room to the garage.

Chapter Three

We cruise around the 610 Loop and head out towards the North side of town. Hauling ass at about a hundred miles an hour, we goof around swapping lanes. His Suzuki is hard to keep up with, or so he thinks. His blond hair gusts in the wind from the speeds we're going. Mine swings around and whips me in the face. I lower my visor to stop the wind lashes that lick the side of my cheek. It's almost midnight, and no traffic.

I throttle down, as we approach the steep left hand turn to the entrance of I-45. Halfway through the curve Dax cranks it back up. I follow.

I crank it back up, and let my Night Rod pass him before we ever hit Crosstimbers or Tidwell Drive. He revs it up and we blast through the Greenspoint Mall-Beltway 8 exit.

It's time to show him what my bike is made of. Let me rip this out. I jam his ass out and scoot him in my dust. I have no idea where we're going, but who cares. This is a blast. I haven't been midnight riding in a long time. I throttle down and look in the rearview mirror. He gives me a 'fuck off dude' grin. Aaron used to worry too much; he didn't do bikes at all. He was a bit twinkish when it came to things like this.

I let Dax speed past me. He grinds it down near the exit ramp to 1960, and hits the right hand turn lane to exit. I jump behind and coast it down to speed limit rules. We exit and hang a sharp right U-turn under the freeway and hit the entrance ramp. As we approach the 610 Loop again, I yank the handlebars towards the right, but sit upright for balance and so I don't tip the bike completely on its side and send myself barreling across the lanes. I can do without a severe case of road rash! I head for home and Dax follows. We pull back in my driveway and I kill the motor.

"I'm impressed." He nods his head towards my bike. "You really do know how to ride Damien."

"Yep, come on in." I'm proud, and impressed that he's impressed.

Dax follows me into the house, and I pull off my jacket and hang it on the hook in the entry hallway. I take Dax's also and hang it up too.

"You want a drink?" I stroll over to my bar.

"Might as well. Hey if it's okay, I'll come by Sunday and shock the pool for you."

"Sounds great. Just whenever you have time. Not like I'll have to drag Aaron out of it this time. In fact I won't ever have to do that again."

Dax reaches out and takes the drink I just poured for him and sits on the couch, taking a sip. I sit down next to him and notice he's staring at me.

"Anything wrong Dax?"

"I knew he was trouble." He looks down at the floor.

"Who Aaron? What do you mean you knew?"

"I come every week to do the pool, you know that. There was a time a couple of weeks ago, that he was outside with someone else."

"What do you mean 'with' someone else?"

"I mean someone who wasn't you Damien." Dax shifts sideways, not wanting to make eye contact with me after letting that one out.

"That mother fucker. Why didn't you say something to me?"

"It's not any of my business. It's not like they were all over each other or anything, but they were flirting. I just figured he was a friend. I didn't think Aaron had big enough gonads to bring someone else in on your home. In case you haven't noticed, you're a pretty scary looking guy sometimes."

"Me scary? How do you figure that?" Curious, I turn to face him.

"Dude, you're tall, you've sleeved out in tats, and you look like you hit the gym ten times a day. You have that air of intimidation all over you, kind of like a biker almost."

"Wow, well not sure I've ever been told that before."

I tip my glass up and down the last bit of drink. I find what he said almost flattering, in a roundabout twisted kind of way. Not that I like being told I look like a biker bully but that he noticed I keep in shape.

"You know I'm a real nice guy right?" I wiggle my eyebrows at him.

"Yes I know, Damien. Look I'm sorry about you and Aaron though."

"Shit happens. So what happened with you and Marcy? Did you find out who the dude was or did she try to explain it?"

"It was her ex." He kicks up one leg, resting it on his other knee. "He came back to town over a month ago, and she wanted to give it another try, so I was out and he was in." His foot is shaking back and forth, he's uncomfortable.

"Damn! You were living with her at her apartment, right?"

"Yep. Mind if I pour another?"

I hold my hand out as a welcome invitation.

He points toward the bottle. "You want one?"

I hand him my glass. "So where are you staying now Dax?"

"Here and there. A spent a couple nights back at home, but that didn't work out so well. I've been at a couple different hotels, I go wherever is close to the job."

"That sucks. If you need a place, I've got three rooms here that I don't use." I wave my hand out in front of me like I'm displaying the house. "You're more than welcome to one of them. I've been debating if I wanted to rent out one or two of them, but I didn't want some stranger in here."

"Really? That would be badass. When I can get a day off, I'll go look for a place of my own." Dax runs his hands through his hair, his eyebrows dip into a furrow. "I won't ever be put in this situation again, this time I'll buy my own place. Business is good, I can afford it." He sits up and turns to me.

"I understand. I feel the same way, and that is why I own this house to be honest. I've been in your shoes and it sucks. You sure you don't mind sharing a home, with me being gay and all that?

"That kind of shit doesn't bother me at all Damien, it never has."

"Good to know, not everyone your age can hack it. How old are you anyway?" He seems so cool about this, not like most people.

"Twenty-four, and you?"

"Coming up on thirty in another month. Not looking forward to that one."

"Me either," he laughs, "I'll go get my things tomorrow morning, my first client isn't until noon."

"Cool. Let me show you the rooms, and you can pick any one you like." I stand, and wait for him to do the same.

"I really appreciate this Damien." He reaches out to shake my hand.

We head upstairs, and Dax looks into the rooms. He ends up picking the one across from mine, it's the biggest and has a view of the backyard. He pulls out his wallet and tries to hand me money, but I make him put it away. Right now I could just use the company more than anything else. Plus I don't mind having live man-candy roaming around the house.

I run back downstairs and get Aaron's old door key for Dax. I lock up the house for the night and set the silent alarm. This living arrangement is going to be very interesting.

Chapter Four

Granger's cold, wet nose presses against my cheek, waking me up.

"All right boy, all right. You need to go outside, don't cha boy?" I reach over and give him a pat.

Granger starts spinning in a circle. I swear he thinks he's a tiny Chihuahua. I climb out of bed, and head downstairs. The smell of sizzling bacon wafts through the air, and my stomach growls. I open the patio door for Granger.

It's a nice cool morning, so I leave the door open. I glance at the wall clock, it reads eight o'clock in the morning. I go in the kitchen, and Dax is standing over the stove. He's got on shorts, but no shirt. *Good gawd...lipsmack!*

The muscles in his back are rigid, tight and firm, like a Greek sculpture. His body frays out, from his waist up to his armpits. His long hair is tossed to one side, and the ridge from his neck down bulges out. *This man is a walking hard-on!*

"Morning Dax."

"Good morning, hope you're hungry?" He turns, giving me a sexy grin.

"Yes, it smells great."

"Oh I forgot to mention, I love to cook," he laughs.

"That's great because I don't, unless it's on the grill outside." I put my hands in the air, giving a visual apology.

He turns the stove off and pulls biscuits from the oven. We have a seat at the table and enjoy breakfast. This is way better than my normal morning. I usually grab something from a drive-thru on the way into work. Aaron didn't cook, he liked me taking him out. He was spoiled.

"So what's on your agenda for today Damien?"

"Oh not much, just a little laundry is all. Think I'll chill out by the pool, and read a bit."

"I wouldn't have figured you for a reader." He takes a sip of his coffee.

"No? I love reading, but hardly ever have time for it anymore, not with work all the time. What do you like to do in your spare time?"

"I rarely have spare time, but I like to bowl, and I love going out to the races at Houston Motor Speedway. When I can, I catch a concert or movie every now and then too. Or cook."

"Well you won't hear me complaining about your cooking from me. The kitchen is yours, so you do with it whatever you wish. I'll give you some money for groceries." Excellent, home cooked meals will be nice for a change.

"Nah, don't worry about it man. You're letting me stay here, the least I can do is pick up the grocery tab. I'll help pitch in on the utilities around here too."

"Sounds like a plan, we'll get it all down on a rental agreement or something later on, no hurry. You heading out to pick up your things this morning?"

"Yes, I have to run over to my parent's house to get my truck. I'll load up a few things, but I should be back in a few hours. Awe crap, I have that job at noon today too. I guess I'll just drop off my things and then go take care of that. Once it's done, besides your pool, I'll be off for the weekend. I can't even remember the last time I had a weekend off."

"You have a good one then, and I'll see you when you get back."

"Laterzzz."

Dax is up and out the door in fifteen minutes. I throw in a load of laundry, and clean up my bedroom. I really need to get a maid in here. That was one good thing about Aaron, he did keep a clean house. Ugh, I need to quit thinking about him, we're done.

I pull out the yellow pages and make a few calls. The maid starts next week on Thursday. *Excellent.*

I change into my bathing suit, open up the doors and windows, and grab my book.

***

"Dude, wake up man." Dax stands over me, holding a beer.

"What, what is it?" I rub my eyes. *Ouch!*

"You are sunburned big time. You fell asleep."

"Shit, what time is it Dax?" I damn near throw myself out of the chair trying to sit up straight.

"Three in the afternoon dude. I just got in from my job."

"Damn, I was beat. I guess it finally caught up with me."

I touch all over my face, but nothing hurts too badly. Good thing I was already halfway tan, or I'd be blistered from head to toe. I dive in the pool to cool off. Dax plunges in behind me.

"Funny being on this side of the water," Dax laughs.

"Yeah it is."

We both swim laps for about twenty minutes, then climb in the hot tub.

"Man, I remember being in these many times, back when I was in high school."

"Been in few, in my days too."

"Can I ask you something Damien?" He rubs his thumb across his chin.

"Go for it."

"Have you ever been with a woman before?" He ducks his head down after asking.

I almost choke. "Yes Dax, many times. Why do you ask?"

"Just curious is all. I mean, when you lived in your other place, I never saw you with anyone, but since being here, you were with Aaron. I just assumed you'd always been gay. So what happened?"

"What happened?" I laugh, "Nothing happened. I've just broadened my horizons is all. Why not try it all, you know?"

"Um…no, I don't know." His expression, one eyebrow arched and mouth dropped wide open, makes me want to laugh. He totally doesn't get it.

"I'll try to explain it, if I can. I go either way. I've never fallen in to any type of stereotypical role. It's like having a lick of all the flavors in an ice cream shop. I think it all comes down to compatibility and communication. When two people click, they just click. It has nothing to do with what they have in their pants. At least not to me. I have girl and guy friends, and I've had both sexually too. No big deal."

"Cool way of looking at it, I guess. I never thought too much about it before. Hey, you feel like doing the bowling thing?" He changes the subject quickly.

"Sure, it's been a while, but why not. I have nothing else planned, and it's still early enough, we can get there before all the Saturday night kids get there."

"Ha, you were one of those kids back in the day too? A bowling alley was the easiest place to score booze. I remember well."

"Yes it was."

I laugh and climb out of the hot tub, wrapping the towel around me and go upstairs to rinse off. I toss on a pair of button up Levi's and throw on a Metallica concert shirt.

Sitting on the side of the bed, I tie up my shoes. Dax and I seem to be hitting it off fairly well. He's really easy to talk to and we seem to have the same interests.

I glance across the hallway, harmless. Dax walks out with a towel around him, and drops it to the floor. He's naked as a jaybird. *Holy mother of HAWT!* He reaches into the closet fumbling for his clothes. His ass is tight like a fucking Gladiator, and the way he just dangles in the wind…whew!

My mouths drops open. I think I've shredded through the studs on the way down to the first floor! ~picks carpet fibers from teeth~

I rub my hand across my dick and it immediately begins to swell beneath my jeans. It throbs so hard, there is no way I can go out without a severe case of blue balls. The sight of Dax across the hall naked is making me shitfuck horny. I've never reacted this way, been able to look at someone and get all hard like this, but with him it's happening. Dax walking around his room naked is fucking incredible, he's got the hottest body I've ever seen. I would give anything just to be able to touch him, to stroke him. I squeeze myself trying to break the spell he's caused on my cock, but it's not working. The throbbing pulsates deep into me and I slowly massage across the bulge in my jeans, I need a release. I slowly unzip my jeans, edging the tip of my cock to freedom. I take my fingers and massage the tip of it. *Oh yeah!*

Dax has his radio blasting, thank God because I can't help but moan. He bends over and towel dries his long hair. *Holy fuck!* His door is only cracked, but it's enough for me to admire the scenery.

My dick grows between my fingertips, and I slip my hand inside my boxers. *Oh fuck me!* God, I hope he doesn't look out the door and see me. I feel like a voyeur, but how can I even resist this. I pop my cock out of my boxers and wrap my hand around it, stroking up and down myself. Thinking about him stroking me occupies my thoughts, that and him walking around his room naked. Damn! I swipe up and down on myself, slow then speeding so I don't get caught. Oh shit, I'm going to come all over myself. I grip tighter, reaching for the lube on the night stand, and squirt a little into my hand. *Oh yesss!* My dick gets to the point of volcanic eruption, and I have to get up and walk into my bathroom, but not before taking another look across the hallway, seeing his tight ass and those legs that don't quit.

I never release myself as I walk into the shower area and close the door. I lean up against the wall, letting my jeans drop to my kneecaps. Furiously, I jack myself hard and quick. My eyes roll back into my head and the image of Dax's swinging cock floods my memory. I'd gladly lower myself to my knees, and suck him into my mouth. I'd love to have him pumping and jutting himself into my mouth, in and out. I'd love to trace my tongue across his balls, licking them towards my mouth, and sucking each one so gently. *Oh my god!*

I press my shoulders against the wall, aiming my groin forward, and slip my hand up and down myself. Imagining him in front of me as I fuck his mouth is almost too much for me to handle. I knee wiggle my jeans down to my ankle, and clench my nuts with my left hand. Jiggling the softness, they begin to tighten. I pump from the tip of my dick down the shaft and slam into my pubic hair, I can stop jerking myself. I tense as my body begins to warm and tingle, the hairs to attention across every part of my body. I lean further out, just like I was ramming myself into his mouth, when I feel the warm release oozing between my fingers. *Oh fuck yes, yess!* The warm jizz splatters into my hands and I gasp for air. He was just the best non-touching fuck I've ever had in my entire life. I pant, trying to regain my composure. Once I come to my senses, I turn the knob on the shower and rinse my hand off. How the hell can someone be the best orgasm ever when you never even touched them? Fucking insane!

Chapter Five

We get in two games here at Diamond Bowl, before all the local teenagers start coming in. We decide to leave, but Dax wants to stop by the grocery store. I haven't been to a grocery store in a year, this should be interesting.

"What are you in the mood for Damien?" Dax turns to me.

"Anything is fine with me, you're the Julia Childs of the house. I'll eat pretty much everything, except liver and beets."

"How about we pick up some fresh veggies, a few top sirloins, and some chicken breasts? We can toss it on the grill, but I'll need some marinade also."

"I'm just here for the ride, whatever you think we need."

I still have no earthly idea what he's making, but who cares, I'm not cooking it. He gets everything, including salad dressing, and beer, we head to the checkout counter. I go ahead of him to load everything into my truck, and he follows me after paying. We head for home.

Pushing the remote to my garage door opener, I pull in remembering that I forgot to get Aaron's clicker. *Shit!* I help Dax with the groceries and we go into the kitchen.

I head upstairs, change clothes and head back downstairs.

"Do you need any help with anything? Damn, I can't believe that just came out of my mouth." I slap my hand across my mouth, joking with him.

"Why?"

"I'm just not in familiar in this part of the house at all. Throw me in the office or out on the site, and I'm at home. But this unchartered part of the house is foreign to me, except for the coffee pot. Now I can cook a mean pot of coffee."

"Cook? That would be brew, right?" Dax laughs. "Do you have any skewers?"

"I have no idea, look through the drawers. What are you concocting in here anyway?"

Dax spreads the sirloins in a pan, pouring beer over them, then puts chicken in another pan, and pours Italian dressing all over it. He covers both pans with foil, and then drinks the rest of the beer. He dumps the vegetables in the sink.

"Concocting? Sounds like a science project. I'm making supper. Do you like shish kebobs?"

I pop the top on a cold one, how do I resist this? "What's not to like about meat on a stick?" I wink.

He spews beer all in the sink from laughing, "Damn Damien, are trying to kill a guy here or what?"

"Sorry, couldn't help myself." I'm practically falling out laughing now.

"Now that was a good one, but you caught me way off guard. Shit!"

We both crack up. I have to admit, he's got a great personality, and thank goodness, a sense of humor. At least he took it in stride. I love his laugh, it's genuine and real. You can tell a lot about a person by their laugh, what they laugh at and how they do it. His is radiating security, confidence and comfort. All great qualities in a person.

"Damien, would you mind firing up the pit? I need to get these vegetables clean." He looks over his shoulder. I love the way he can raise one eyebrow.

"No problem."

I walk out by the pool to start the grill, and I light the tiki torches. I love the essence of grilling food, and the whole outdoor cooking ambiance.

Dax comes out with the trays of meat and place the food on the pit. He sets the tray on top of the sink in the covered mini bar next to the pool.

"I'm going to run up and change myself now, be right back."

Is he wearing a diaper or something? I laugh at the way he words things, I think he meant change clothes. I grab us a couple of the beers from the mini fridge, then return to the patio table.

"Much better, man I love this time of year in Texas."

"You and me both. So you're off work tomorrow?"

"Yep, don't have another job until Monday at lunchtime." Dax stretches his arms back. "All of my clients seem to sleep late for some reason. I think most of them smoke a little too much herb sometimes."

"I could probably get you some business with some of the people at my work. Make sure you give me some business cards."

"I'd appreciate that man. So how are things on your side of work?" He takes a swallow of his beer.

"Going good. I've got to be on the site Monday morning, we're setting up to do some more repairs on I-10."

"Will that interstate ever be done? As long as I can remember, it's always been under repairs."

"You sound like the reporter that keeps giving us flack about that." I laugh. "We take it in sections, and so many factors play into that, it's insane."

"I can imagine." He lights up a smoke. "Want one?"

"Yes, I left mine upstairs."

I spark up, and he turns the kabobs over. Granger runs up to him, sniffing the air.

"Hey there boy, I wondered where you were, you big mutt." He pets him on the back, rubbing up and down his fur. "Does he ever go swimming with you?"

"In my old place he did, but he's never been in this pool."

"Need another beer?"

I nod, and he walks over to get one, and places it in my hand.

"I can't believe you aren't out here every night, making use of all this."

"I think I used it once or twice, maybe. I guess I was just too busy getting everything else around here organized." I was too busy catering Aaron's ass around town actually.

"Bet it was an adjustment. This place is much bigger than your old one."

"A lot bigger, but I'm comfortable here, you know? This place feels like home. The other one never did."

"Hell, I just got here, and it feels like home. Oh shit, the food."

He jumps up and rushes to the pit, pouring his beer on the coals to lower the flame, and I bolt to the bar to get a glass of water just in case. Filling the glass, he comes into the bar area, squishing in front of me to get the tray. The flame is out. His ass rubs up against me, and instinctively my free hand reaches to his hipbone, giving a gentle squeeze.

Dax glances back towards the grill to make sure the flame is out. I know I should jerk my hand away, but I can't move. He's not moving either. Neither of us says a word.

Dax inhales a deep breath, and leans back slightly, against me. It seems like ten minutes has past, but realistically I know it's only been a few seconds.

I inhale his cool water cologne, my god he smells fucking good. I lean forward just a bit, and brush my lips across his bare back. His skin is warm from him working in the sun all the time. I continue sliding my lips across the curves in his back. His skin breaks out in goose bumps, but he still doesn't move away.

With the tip of my tongue, I make little swipes at his skin, and he gasps again. I slide my left hand from his hipbone to the front a tiny bit, and my finger slips inside the top of his waistband of his shorts. He shifts, so I remove it, but still caress his stomach muscles in my palm.

Dax lets out a quiet moan, "Mmm…"

I let out a groan at the feel of all those muscles. My lips pucker and I begin giving him pecks to his back, followed by my swirling tongue, tracing across to another area. He presses just a little harder back against me, still holding the tray in his hands. He tosses his head back towards me, engulfing my face in long blond strands.

I lower my hand, gliding across his cotton shorts and into his cargo pocket. With my index finger, I trace up and down against his dick in his pants, he's hard. Closing my fingertips together, I pinch through the material, and slide up and down his cock. A loud breath escapes from him again, and I breathe into his back, causing chill bumps to explode all over him.

He moans, and then turns sideways towards the grill.

"Shit, the food."

He pushes back towards me with his ass, and I move back quickly, as he darts back to pull the food from the flames that just sparked up again.

Chapter Six

This is just a tad bit awkward. It's more like I'm a little on the freaked out side. I'm not sure how to handle, or deal with what happened with Damien, or the strange silent dinner we just had. After we finish, I clean up, go to my room and plop down on my bed. I cross my hands behind my head, trying to wrap my brain around what happened.

Did Damien touching me, make me horny? Hell yes. Did it scare the living crap out of me? Fuck yeah. Did I want Damien to stop? Yes. Did I want him to continue? Absolutely. Now, how do I even begin to sort this out, when all I can do is contradict myself and my thoughts?

I've never even thought about being with a man. For starters, I've never had to deal with anything even close to this. When I was a kid, it was all about the chicks. It always has been, and guys have never once entered into it, not ever. The stereotypical things come into play about dudes, they are your hanging out buddies, your kick it around crew. This is how I was raised.

So why didn't I stop Damien from touching me? God, I have to hash this all out in my head. Not knowing why I feel a certain way about something is making me mental.

I like the fact that Damien's just an overall cool dude. He's funny and easy to get along with. Damien isn't the kind of guy to prance around throwing his opinions on everyone. He's a self-confident man, secure in his life, cocky when it comes to business, successful, intelligent, fun and easy going. And the man, I'm certain, has never pranced a day in his life. He's manly, a bit rugged, and he definitely has that whole bad-boy thing going on.

Is there anything not likeable about Damien? I don't think so. He's not mean or arrogant, and he's not a woman hater. He's just a man who explores all flavors of things, as he said.

I think the reason this scares me so bad, is because of all the stereotypes, and to be honest, I'm not ready to face it. I've never held anything against a person before, and certainly don't judge people. I take people at face value, and accept everyone's right to be themselves. Everyone has their own opinions and expressions, they're allowed to be who they are. I've never understood people who do these kinds of things to another human being. It's what makes us all unique as people, different, but there is always someone out there who is ready to bash someone else, without regard for the persons' feelings. It's never made sense to me, are they all out to hide their own insecurities, and boost their own egos. It's ridiculous.

Now the real question, the one my mind doesn't even want to think about is did I like it? The way he feels, the way he makes me feel? It did feel good. The physical feeling itself isn't any different than being touched by a woman. It's a bit shocking at first, but in those few minutes, or seconds, not sure which, my mind didn't focus on the obvious.

Damien's kisses were warm, even passionate. I still broke out in goose bumps the way I've always done when turned on. Maybe his hands were rougher, I don't recall. My body responded to his caresses the same way they always have. In those few minutes, everything was great in my book, it seemed normal. Sensual, and somewhat erotic too.

So what is it I'm so scared of again? Is it just the idea of it all being different because he's a man, or is it because I'm worried I'll get hurt again? Both! There were two people in my past that hurt me, and I've pretty much written off anything serious with anyone since.

The first was a girl named Carrie. I really fell hard for her, head over heels in love, but she didn't quite feel the same. She loved me, but after a year and a half, she moved on, and I was left to try to pick up shattered pieces of my heart that she left trailing after her. It was hard, I'm not even sure to this day that I've completely gotten past her, I'm not sure that's even possible, but I just adapted. I'd always promised myself I wouldn't get involved that deeply with anyone ever again, and I haven't.

The other person is my brother, Dale. We were close, tighter than most. We did almost everything together, except for that one night. If I had been there, my brother would still be alive.

So yes, the fears of this whole situation with Damien, catches me on two sides, both resulting in hurt. The fear of loss, maybe. When I get too close to things they disappear, so I try to keep myself from that. Is that what this is all about?

Shit, maybe it really is, but now the question comes back around to the obvious. Is taking this any further with Damien even an option for me? I don't know, I honestly just don't know.

For two reasons, this needs to get resolved. One, I need to know what he's thinking about it all, and the second reason is that since I'm now living here, things could go south quick if it's not straightened out.

I need to talk to him!

Chapter Seven

After the uneasy way things ended between Dax and me, I'm not sure what to think. I know I was probably out of line with what happened, but it just kind of happened. It wasn't my plan to grope all over him like a stray cat in heat. What was I thinking? Dax, and I haven't talked about it, we pretended it didn't happen, but it made everything very awkward. The silent dinner was horrible.

I'm not sure how to act, what to say. It's not like I can walk up him, and say *'Geez, Dax. Thanks for letting me cop a feel on your junk last night, you're a real pal.'* God, I need coffee bad. *Someone shoot me!*

Downstairs, I let Granger out, and continue my mission to find caffeine. I've got a hangover from hell, my head is throbbing. As I round the corner to the kitchen, I run smack-dab into Dax.

"Oh, crap...sorry man." I step to the side.

"My fault." Dax sidesteps too, his expression full of shock.

After last night, he probably thinks I'm about to hit my knees for an encore performance. We both move, but in same direction. *Oh god!* Face to face, we block one another's path again.

"Sorry. I need coffee bad." I smile and choke at the same time.

"Ditto, I just made us a fresh pot."

"Thanks." I wave my hand for him to pass.

He looks relieved as he passes me. Ugh, I hate these kinds of moments, when everything is out of whack, strange, and flat out awkward. I pour a cup and head outside for the newspaper.

After retrieving, I sit on the couch, putting my coffee down on the table. Dax is in the recliner by the fireplace. I flip through the paper, not really looking for anything in particular, except the forecast.

"Ah hell."

"Something wrong, Damien?" He leans forward in his chair, glancing my way.

"Storms are coming through the next couple days. A hundred percent chance of rain this afternoon, plus the next two days." I toss the paper on the couch. I rub my hands over my face. "Guess that will shut down my work for the next week or so, until it dries up."

"Seriously, storms? I guess that means I'll be off too. I better get busy reschedule everything." He stands up, looks out the window, and takes his cell from the end table.

"I need to call the foreman on each of the sites, and check in with the office." I stand and walk upstairs.

Work wise, this isn't what I need right now, but I can't control Mother Nature. The reporters are going to have a field day, again. At least now, I can take a few days off.

After spending three hours calling everyone, I finally peel my ear from the phone and head back downstairs.

"Did you get all your calls taken care of?"

"Yes, finally, and I took off a few days while at it. I think the last day I had off was this time a year ago. Granger needs shots, plus I need to get all my tax info together." I wipe the sweat from my brow.

"I'm headed over to my parents, kind of our Sunday thing to have lunch, but I'll be back tonight. Need anything while I'm gone?"

"No thanks, I'm good."

"Okay Damien, enjoy your day." He turns to walk away, but glances back.

"Hey, did you want to ride? You're more than welcome to come with me."

I'm good. But hey, thanks, I appreciate it." He digs through the basket, grabs his keys and strolls out the door.

I'm surprised he asked, that was pretty cool of him. At least it temporarily broke the ice for a few minutes. My house phone rings, and I snatch it up, only seeing the caller ID afterward. It's Aaron.

"Hi," he says.

"What Aaron?" I clench the phone, I'm going to end up shattering it, I swear.

"I just wanted to see if you were okay."

"I'm fine. I need the clicker for the garage door."

"Oh sorry, I forgot to give it back. I left a few things in the garage too. I'll come by in a couple hours, all right?"

"Yeah, fine Aaron." I slam the phone down.

I don't want to talk to Aaron, much less see him, but I also don't want him having a way inside my home when I'm not here. That trust is shot to shit. I try to be a forgiving and caring person, sometimes that's just impossible. Especially in a situation like this.

Thunder booms, and the crack of lightning snaps across the sky like a Dom's whip. Dark gray clouds roll over the blue sky, as sporadic bolts detonate the skyline with light. The bottom's about to fall out, so I run out to throw a few things in the mailbox, and let Granger piss before the storm hits. When I stroll back inside, the scent of Dax's cologne radiates off of his jacket that hangs by the front door.

I flash back to what's happened in the short time he's been here. I honestly hope we can get past things, I never meant to make him skittish or uncomfortable around me. He's just a good, down to earth man, I was way off base by letting my alcohol take over me the way it did.

Although I would love things to go further, I'll have to keep him in his mind. Just thinking of him makes me horny. The way he walks, and laughs. His smile is so sexy. *Fuck me.* I lay on the couch, feeling the tingle in my cock. I slip my jogging pants over my dick, wrapping my hand around it. As I think of him, and his pouty lips, I stroke up and down on my shaft imaging the way it felt with him leaning back against me, as I slithered my hands across his chest. I pump harder, and faster. I imagine what it would have been like to be him over and sink my dick into him. Oh yeah… I start breathing harder. Faster and faster, I jerk my dick knowing I'm about to cum. I close my eyes, and imagine fucking him in the mouth. *Yesss.* I cream all over my sweats.

***

A hairy nudge against my face wakes me up. I try to push Granger out of my face. When I shove him, I snap to full alert. It's Aaron.

"What the hell? Get away from me!" My feet scramble to find a grip so I can push myself up straight.

"Hey you."

He leans towards me, but I push him away. The room swirls back into focus. I fell asleep on the couch. What is he doing here? Wait…

"How the fuck did you get in my house?" I jump up off the couch, and stare at him.

"The garage door."

"Hand it over Aaron, now!"

"What? Are you trying to tell me we're done, after the time we spent together? Seriously Damien?"

I hold out my hand and wave my fingertips towards me, giving him the 'hand it to me now' motion. Aaron slams the clicker in my palm. He's pissed, but I'm beyond that right now.

"Get your stuff out of my garage, then go." I cross my arms across my chest.

"Fine!" Aaron peacocks towards the front door, and then spots it.

"Who the fuck does this belong too?" He picks up Dax's jacket off the hook.

I point at the door. "Leave Aaron."

Aw hell! I see the front door knob turn. Dax walks in. His eyebrows pinch in the middle, and his lips thin as he looks down on Aaron. This just turned serious, real quick like.

"Not until you tell me who this belongs too."

Dax towers over Aaron, his hand reaching out for his jacket.

"This…belongs to me." Aaron tilts his head up towards Dax.

"What? Wait, how did you get in here, the door was locked? I tried it from outside."

"My key." He dangles it in the air, giving him a shit-eating grin. "Damien, is everything okay here?"

"Yes, Aaron came to drop of…"

58

"Oh, I remember, he has my garage door remote right?" He gives me a wink, assuring me that he's got control of the situation.

"Um…yes, it's here." I hold out my hand, showing him.

"What the hell is going on Damien?" Aaron's eyes dart back and forth from me to Dax.

"Don't see how any of that is your business anymore Aaron, now is it?"

If looks could kill, I'd be pushing up daisies about now from the look Aaron just gave me.

"You hypocritical cockfag." Aaron grits his teeth. "Let me tell you both something you worthless…"

"Look twatwaffle, you need to get out of Damien's house, now."

Dax places his hand against the small of Aarons back, guiding him towards the door.

"Take your fucking hands off me." Aaron, lunges away from him, and throws his hands up in the air.

Dax ushers him out the door, while I pick my mouth up off the floor. Damn, damn! I didn't mean for all that to happen, this is not good.

I follow them outside, taking my stance next to Dax. I'm not even sure what to say. He lights up a smoke. We watch, as Aaron puts two boxes in his truck. He flips us the bird, shredding rubber down the street.

"Dude, man I'm sorry Damien. I know it wasn't my place at all to do that, but the man has no right to question you in your own home."

"I know. Sorry you walked in on that. I wasn't planning to let him in the house, but I fell asleep and he came in through the garage door."

"Sneaky little bastard, isn't he?" He elbows me in the side.

"Like a rattlesnake hidin' in grass."

Dax laughs and we walk back into the house.

Chapter Eight

I glace at the clock and it's almost two o'clock in the afternoon. This morning after Dax and I did our morning kitchen tango dance around each other, followed by our silent coffee conversation, I'd come into my room to shower, and get busy on my IRS files, and now I'm finally finished.

As I exit the room, smack…straight into Dax. This is the third time now already. Enough! I open my mouth, but he speaks first.

"How long do you reckon we're going to do this tap dance around each other?" He puts his hands on his hips.

"I was beginning to wonder the same thing. I think we need to get past this already."

"Let's go grab a beer."

I follow him into the kitchen, and he pulls out two beers. The phone rings, but by the time I get there, they've hung up. Caller ID show unknown caller.

"I apologize for what happened out by the pool the other night. I was way out of line, and I feel like a complete asshole." I slide out the kitchen chair, and have a seat. "I was half drunk, which is not an excuse, but I went all cockfangled on you, and I'm really sorry. I don't want to ruin our friendship and I'm afraid I have." I talk with my hands, and it looks like

I'm throwing gang signs or something. I decide to sit on them instead.

"Cockfangled?" He lights up a smoke, and passes me the pack.

"Complicated and convoluted. Believe me, I didn't mean to cross the invisible line of friendship." I take the lighter off the table and spark up my own.

"Okay, apology accepted. Can we just ta-talk now Damien? In case you didn't notice, I wasn't exactly going ballistic about bein-being touched," he stutters.

"I noticed, but Dax, you were pretty buzzed."

"The fact re-remains that I didn't bolt when it happ-ened." Nonchalantly, he takes a swallow of beer, holding up his finger. "Don't say anything, and let me get this out p-please."

I nod, taking another puff on my smoke.

"I need to calm down so I q-quit this stuttering crap." He takes a deep breath. "Okay, sorry. What I'm trying to say is the reason I didn't turn around and punch you is because it felt good. You felt good."

"Whoa. Wait, what?" I take another long drag on my smoke.

"Listen Damien, I've run this wh-whole situation through my mind, over and over, and come to a conclusion."

"Okay, I'm listening." *What is he talking about?*

"It felt good and I think I'm okay with that. I'm not sure why, but maybe you can help me sort all this out, there are so many things I'll be sorting anyway.

I'm going to be completely honest with you okay?" He looks at me, and I nod yes. "It's not the fact that you touched me, or the fact that I en-enjoyed it. That is something I'll have to figure out or we will. It's the matter of me having issues with relationships."

"You did? I mean you do?" *Shit, now I'm having brain stutters.* "Let me start over, one thing at a time. You enjoyed me touching you?" I shift in my chair, sitting up straight, and take a swallow of my beer.

Dax's hands squirm together, fumbling over each other. He's nervous, so I reach over to give a friendly, reassuring pat on top of his clasped hands. He opens them quickly, taking my hand. He gives me such a shy grin, but it's cute. I can feel the twinge in my groin. *I never saw this one coming.*

"Tell me, about the issues with relationships." *God, I sound like fucking Dr. Phil.*

"I don't do them well. I've learned that when you let things in, or too close, they get messed up." He lowers his head to our hands and rests against them.

"I understand to a certain point. In other words, you're human."

"I wish it was that easy. I keep people at an arms' length distance for their protection and mine alike."

"Are you talking about Marcy?"

"No not Marcy. That wasn't a big deal, I figured it was going no-where quick, so I didn't emotionally attach or anything like that. Have you ever been in love Damien?"

63

"Yes, once. Why?"

"How did you feel about him, didn't you want to give your all to him? Then feel betrayed at some point, that you did that?"

"First off, he was a she. I was married once Dax, her name was Nickie. We divorced four years ago. I was married for three. I get being in love. I was head over heels with Nickie, and had my heart broken when she decided she wanted a divorce. Hell thinking about it now still hurts."

"I just assumed…"

"That I have always been gay?" I shake my head side to side and give him a sly grin.

"Well, yes." He squirms in his chair.

"I'm bisexual. There was only one wife, and two men. One lasted about a week, the other was Aaron not lasting much longer. I told you, I've licked the flavors of life."

"My first love was a girl named Carrie. It lasted about a year and a half, but I'm still not sure if I've gotten past her emotionally."

"I'm sorry Dax." I squeeze his hand tighter.

"Thank you. The other person, the one thing that hurt worse than anything in my life, is my brother, Dale."

"What happened?"

Dax pulls his hand back from my grip, takes a drink and lights up a smoke. I light another cigarette too and wait until he's ready to talk. Dax is sizing me up and down in his mind, I feel it.

"My brother was my best friend. I should have been with him and everything might have been so different."

Dax's face turns red, and he takes several quick draws on the cig, like a chain smoker. After, he inhales a couple long deep breaths. He begins to speak again.

"We had a thing about going muddin' down at Spring Creek. We'd always done it, since back when we were in high school, everyone did. One Saturday night, I had a date, and blew him off. Dale, and one of our friends, went to the creek without me." He inhales a long, hard drag. "They were drinking, everyone did when they went bogging. They crossed down the paths through the woods that led to the creek. When they got there, they saw another four wheel drive, stuck out in the sand barge in the creek. Of course Dale backed up to the guys, hooking up the 'come-along' to the dude's bumper and yanked him out. The guys were happy and appreciative, so they all sat down, and had a couple beers together."

With another drag, he snubs his smoke out in the ashtray. "Young, drunk guys do what most drunk guys do, talk shit. Dale got an earful, and he got up and went to untie all the straps then come home. His buddy helped him. Dale never saw it coming, the guy punched our friend, and Dale jumped in to help him.

65

Unable to keep his eye on all of the guys at the same time, one of them hit him. He caught a tire iron across his skull, he was killed instantly." Dax tears up.

"Oh God!" *What do I even say to something like that?*

"See that's on me, all of me. If I would have only been there, I could have stopped it." Red-faced, he shakes his head, and flings a tear off of his cheek.

I reach out to him, using my thumb to dry his tear trail. "You don't know that though. You might have been killed too."

"Maybe, but the end result is still the same…pain and hurt. This is why I don't do relationships. When I get close to things, they disappear on me one way or another." He lights another cigarette.

"Dax, damn dude. I'm so sorry, but you have to see everything's not always like that though."

"I don't dare get close enough to find out anymore." He emphasizes his statement by slamming his fist on the table.

"That's not fair." I have to let him know it wasn't his fault, and it's not justifiable to blame it on himself. "It's not fair to you, or too others. You have to get past this Dax, try to deal with it, realize it's not your fault, and try to move forward in life.

This is fucking tragic, so painful. I see a side to him way beyond his normal happy-go-lucky self, and I feel bad for him. I don't know how to help him, or if I even can. I put my cigarette out in the ashtray, and take a sip of beer, hoping that something, anything comes to mind to. Before I can stop myself, the words blurt out.

"Let me help you, at least let me try."

"Help me what?"

"Learn that everything isn't always about pain and hurt."

I stand to go get another beer, Dax does the same. He's staring at me, studying me, but for what I'm not sure. I don't wish harm, and I'm not trying to rush him into anything. He's obviously figured out for himself that he avoids certain things because of the circumstances he's been through.

"Thanks, I appreciate that Damien. I really do. I've never really talked to anyone about this stuff, so I'm not sure why I am now, but thanks for listening."

Dax pats me on the upper part of my arm, and his hand slides down to my elbow. I stare into his dark blue eyes, and notice the black pupil is dilating. *His eyes are soul sucking.*

His fingers begin to squeeze my upper arm, not hard, but in a sensual way. I take a deep breath. My hand in front of me, I touch his stomach. As Dax, massages into my arm, I slide my knuckles across his stomach a bit. Still not sure about what is going on, I wait. I can't be the one to go first this time.

Dax slides his hand up my arm to my shoulder, and I slip my hand to the side of his waist. I squeeze slightly, and he inhales a deep breath again. Fingers trickle to my face, and with the back of his finger, he strokes my cheek. I clasp his side tight. We both drop our heads.

Forehead to forehead, we freeze. As his neck tilts to the side, I pucker. Like iron to a magnet, our necks twist to that special spot, where everything is unknown, but suddenly discovered, and we fit lips together, locking in a rage of passion. Our first kiss...my grip tightens around his waist, pulling him in close.

I trace my tongue over his salty lips, parting them. My tongue nudges inside his mouth, licking the inside of his lips. I circle my tongue around to the top of his dipped lips on his mouth and back down, he darts his tongue to mine. I give him tiny flicks to his tongue, we play follow the leader. When I back away a bit, I feel his tongue hungrily force back into my mouth. I suck the tip, as I feel the wetness slither through my pursed lips. *Fuckin' Tease*!

He sucks my bottom lip between his pouty lips. I feel the tug, the wanting and anxiousness. Teeth graze the top of my lip, as he gently sucks such tender nibbles into him. I pull back, looking at him, and giving him a 'fuck-me-goddamned sideways' grin! His sultry-seductive eyes melt me.

Pressing back against him, I delve into his mouth full force, not gently, but hungrily. My tongue thrashes against his, and I lower my hand to his groin.

Rubbing through the material I can feel him swelling through the denim material. Dax moves his hand to my waist, and stops. I continue kneading him through his jeans, and then back away, waiting. It's his move now.

"Are you okay?" I ask because I'm really concerned.

"Yes."

"Let's go upstairs."

He smiles and closes his eyes. Finally, he nods.

The phone rings, and Dax grabs it.

"Hello? Hello?" He holds the phone out to his side in the air and shrugs his shoulders.

We both look at the caller id…unknown caller. Who keeps calling, bad timing.

Chapter Nine

I've never played the Fairy Godmother before, the tutor so to speak, I'm just as nervous as Dax is. He'll be making his debut, his very first homosexual experience. His comfort level is at the top of my list, I'd never try to pressure him into something he didn't want to try. I've been there, and there wasn't anything nice about it.

I don't play the Alpha/Sub routine. There's nothing wrong with both parties taking turns as Alpha, I find it more appealing, because both lovers get to enjoy all flavors of the rainbow. *I sound like a freaking Starburst commercial.*

As we walk past the bar to the living room, there's a thundering boom outside, and the power zaps. Granger hauls ass up the stairs, I know he's going under my bed. It sounds like the transformer blew down the street. Great! That'll take a few hours to get fixed.

"I need to report this outage, give me a couple minutes."

Dax nods and strolls over to the couch. *Damn, he sure knows how to pack an ass inside those jeans. Geezus!*

After filing the report, I stroll back into the living room. Dax is standing at the back door, watching the rain come down. I set two beers on the table and come up behind him. He jerks. I didn't mean to scare him.

I slip my arms around his waist and snug up on his back. Dax twists to face me. With my fingertips, I skim over his pouty lips, tracing the outline of his curves, and dips. We both stare into each other's eyes. As my finger reaches the bottom lip again, I glide into his mouth. His tongue licks around my finger. All I can imagine is Dax on his knees in front of me. *My dick is so hard, it could bend steel.*

I pull back and walk over to the couch. Dax follows and sits on my left side. He gives me a catch-sexy smile, as I rotate sideways. I see him perfectly now.

As his leg bounces up and down nervously, I place my hand on his thigh. We're stuck in eye-lockdown, neither of us can break it. He radiates heat through the jeans. I part his lips and slip my finger inside his mouth. He curls his tongue around my finger. I pull back but he sucks me back. *God, I want to feel him around my cock.*

I lean my head in close to him and my lips caress against his. Instinctively our mouths open a little. I twine my fingers in his hair, and our tongues swipe together in mid-air. *God he's lickable!*

I tilt my head and deliver baby pecks to his neck. My tongue swirls tiny spheres, he moans. I finger walk up his jeans until I get to his package. Grabbing hold, my hand opens and tightens around his crotch, in a pulsating grip. Not too hard or too easy.

His raging boner strains the zipper in his jeans. That's a feeling I know all too well. I reach for the button and unfasten them, the zipper is next. I release the beast and move my head back to look at his glistening cock. It's beautiful, incredible actually. Dax watches everything I'm doing.

"Are you okay?" I stroke over his cheek with my fingers, offering some kind of re-assurance to him.

"Yes."

"Still nervous?"

"Yep, a li-little, but I'll be all right."

Never missing a beat, my hand hugs around his dick. Hungrily, our mouths widened, and I plunge my tongue deep inside of him. I stroke him. Our tongues thrash in foreplay and our heads twist and turn from side to side. I tug on his bottom lip and suck it into my mouth. He moans, and my cock swells in anticipation, even more at the sound of him, it's like there's a direct link from his moan straight to my prick. I tug on his jeans, and he raises his ass and helps me wiggle them down his legs, and finally all the way off. *He's smokin' hot!*

He pulls his shirt over his head and helps to remove mine. I have to taste him. I want to lick every inch of his fuck hot body and feel him inside my mouth. Dax's entire body erupts in chill bumps, his legs shake a tiny bit. I lick my lips and trace his nipples into tiny peaks with my tongue. I lick my way down his happy trail, lower and lower. Finally, I take his cock in my mouth, making sure to flick my tongue around his bulbous head. In a pucker he slips out and slams back in my mouth.

His hands slither like a snake through my curls, as he clutches me near my scalp. My fingers claw into chest, as he grinds out four pumps into my mouth. I release him from my mouth and crawl down on the floor, spreading his legs apart. My warm tongue laps teasingly at his balls. I reach for his dick again, taking him in my hand.

"Mmm…" I moan between slurping noises.

Dax scoots down, sliding his ass over the edge of couch, as I continue licking at him. I lift his nut sack, and flatten my tongue so I can lap his balls. He lets out another moan. My tongue tickles down his gooch until I reach his crack.

My hands release him, and I scoop my hands up under him, cupping his ass, and gently squeezing. I spread his ass cheeks apart and vibrate my tongue in circles around his recky. I lick my finger and slowly push into him.

"Oh God!" He lets out a long moan. *Or-fucking-gasmic!*

In and out, he moans to both. I want him to have the best fucking orgasm ever. I trace my tongue back to his nut sack, give it a little flick, and take his shaft in my mouth again. My finger wiggles inside his ass, crooking to find his prostate gland.

Dax pants shallow, quick breaths and a deep and raspy moan escapes his lips. I go down on him, taking him deeper into my mouth. He starts thrusting into me, his cock rams the back of my throat, and I almost gag. He's in a frenzy, he squirms and bucks into me, his hands go from my head to my hands, to my cheek and back up. I suck my cheeks in tight, drawing his dick tight into my mouth. Between his moans and his body movements, he's driving me crazy. My dick is so hard right now, I want to start whacking myself off.

"I'm gonna come. Don't stop. Suck me off."

I love him being talkative, telling me what he likes. I swear I'm going to cum all over myself listening to him. I don't dare take my mouth from around his cock. I give him a thumbs up to let him know there is no way I'm stopping now. He digs his fingernails into my back. His whole body starts shaking, and his moaning is deep and raspy. I tighten my jaw as he juts into me quickly. The warm, sticky goo fills my mouth as he explodes into me.

"Ah fuck yes!"

Dax tilts his head back on the couch, breathing heavy. He's got a big smile on his face. Me however, I feel like my dicks going to explode. I wish he'd take me in his mouth, but he hasn't tried to touch me, much less suck me off. He's inexperienced. I'll just have to show some patience and remember the old saying that 'good things come to those who wait.'

I'll wait.

Chapter Ten

Two days has passed since our little 'moment' in the living room. The rain hasn't let up a bit, so I'm taking the week off work. I like being home with Dax. Nothing's been uncomfortable between us this time. I'm trying to give him time to make sure this is still what he wants.

The relationship between us seems to have mellowed out into some sense of normalcy. When we pass each other in the kitchen or hallway, we don't go all Matrix around each other, breaking in to twists and turns like a 'contortionist' in order to avoid touching. The awkward silence is also something of the past. Dax slowly strokes against me, instead of leaping backwards. We've been able to talk, not about anything in particular, but getting to know each other better, and it's been nice to have a companion that you can do that with. We also heist a few kisses throughout the day.

The phone on the nightstand beside the bed rings, I answer.

"Hello?" I wait. "Hello, who is this?"

"I need to talk to you Damien."

"What the hell Aaron, was that you on all the other 'unknown' numbers?" *Get a life!*

"I don't know what you mean. Listen we need to talk, I miss you."

"Not a chance Aaron. There is nothing here for you, not me or any of your belongings, so quit calling me."

"Oh let me guess, you and pool boy have something going on now?"

"If I did, it wouldn't be any of your damn business, now would it?" I start pacing the floor.

"Well, you and your new plaything have fun sitting around playing tiddly winks on each other's tom-toms. Best enjoy it while you can!"

"What the hell is that supposed to mean?"

Aaron laughed. *Click,* he hung up on me. *What the fuck is that all about?* Dax comes out of his room and walks in mine.

"You alright Damien? You don't look so good." His hand strokes through my hair.

"Yeah, I am. You know all those calls from unknown callers? I think its Aaron. I finally answered one and it was him going through the routine," I sigh.

"What routine?"

"The one where he wants to talk to me. He misses me and all that rig-a-maroo. Then I think he threatened me."

"What? What the fuck did he say exactly?" Dax's brows furrow. He practically has steam blowing out his ears. *Dayam!*

"He asked if we were together, I refused to answer and told him none of his business. He told me I best enjoy it while I can." I sit down on the bed.

"Where does the nutlick stay?" Dax walks back and forth in front of me, his boots shredding carpet strands.

"No Dax, leave it alone, he's harmless. Besides, I'm quite capable of taking care of myself."

"Threatening someone is not harmless." Dax sits beside me with his hand on my leg. "I know you can take care of yourself, I didn't mean it like that. Just watch your back. People are crazy." He sits next to me.

"It's just an act, that's all he knows how to do, play fucking games." I look him in the eyes. "You're very sexy when you're mad Dax." I wink, and give him a grin

"Is that right? Hmmm…" Dax licks his lips, and a grin forms in the corner of his mouth.

"Yeah it is right."

"So, what would you recommend as a treatment for anger outbursts?"

I reach out and touch his cheek, then lean into his neck, and begin licking lust all over him.

"Mmm…some of this." I nibble his neck with my teeth, just barely nipping him.

"Uh huh." He tilts his head to the side.

"And a little bit of that." I lick across his lips.

"Oh yes, definitely some of that too."

"Maybe just a tad of this." I rub my hand against his dick, pressing hard into his groin.

"Hell yes, but I need a shower before we carry this any further."

"So, how can I persuade you to let me in the shower with you?" I jokingly ask him.

"I'm not sure, make me an offer?" *There's that sexy eyebrow arch thing he does.*

I part his lips and plunge into his mouth, curling my tongue around his, then pull out. I stand and then straddle his legs, pressing my growing dick against his. "Does this sway you one direction or the other?"

"Oh yeah, it definitely does." He smiles, giving me a quick nip on my lip, followed by a gentle peck.

"Good. We can use mine, it's bigger."

"Is that right?" he laughs.

"Bwahahaha, not that kind of bigger Dax, I was talking about the showers. My 'shower' is bigger than yours. You're adorable."

"Oh, the shower. Yes, that is indeed bigger."

We both go into my bath area and undress. Dax watches me. He's never seen me in my birthday suit. I enter the stall and get my hair wet.

The shower curtain pulls back, and Dax steps in behind me. I hand him the soap. He takes the bar, and begins rubbing it all over me, then passes it to me.

Soft caresses spread across my shoulders and glide down my arms. Once he reaches my fingertips, he slowly wraps his arms around my stomach. The moisture from the showerhead mists on him, bringing his cologne to a refreshed scent, I love his smell of masculinity. I lean back into his blanketed arms and feel his rigid dick pressing against me. *Fuck me now.*

From behind, he grips my chest in his hands, rubbing my tiny nipples. His hands travel from my chest, to my groin. He slips a little lower and runs his long fingers along my happy trail, then continues winding into my curly hairs. *Good god I'm horny!* His hands pull upwards and away from my groin. *Nooo, come back already.*

"Tease!" I reach around and smack him on the leg.

Dax reaches around and snags my ass in his grip. Squeezing, releasing, and squeezing again. I press my ass backwards, and his fingers spread me. His finger tracing around me, then he stops. Almost gasping, his dick presses against me.

"Turn around." He bites into my shoulder, then licks it afterward.

Rock fucking hard, I turn to him. He looks me up and down, with such a bad boy shit-eating grin on his face. *Fuck he's hot!* He attacks my mouth, his tongue plunges in hard, as he laps mine. I press my hands on his chest slamming him into the tile wall. He lets out a groan, I plunge in his mouth, we play tongue twister with the tips of our tongues. I grab his cock in my hands, stroking him fast and furious. He grabs mine, and strokes up and down quickly too.

We jack each other, rotating the head of our dicks together. Dax lifts me up and I saddle his waist, leg locking myself to him. *Goddamn he's strong.* He walks with me and slams my back into the wall. *Paybacks.* I grab his long hair and yank, he devours my mouth.

His hands tighten around my ass cheeks. He pulls and tugs, spreading me. One of his long fingers enters me. *Oh fuckinshit.* In and out, he plunges into me, fucking me with his hand. *Oh god.* I yank his hair tight, like holding reins.

He sets me down on the floor and lowers himself to his knees. Chill bumps erupt and a series of spasms aimed directly at my cock start to tingle. He knocks me in both knees with his hands, so I spread my feet apart. His finger enters my hole again and slips in and out of me. I look down at him and watch what he's doing. *What a fucking sight, him bent down like this.* I love the way my dick causes his cheeks to puff out. Rocking his head with my hands, I speed him up, and push in a little further. He looks up at me. *Fucking hell!* His eyes, oh my god, they're heavy lidded, but incredibly sexy. I pull his head, a little further, in to my dick.

"I'm about to cum Dax. Stop." I push his head back, but he fights me.

"No." He looks up at me, the veins on his neck bulge out.

"Yes, I mean it."

Dax pulls back, sliding his wet skin up against me, and steps out of the shower. He snatches a towel off the hook and wraps it around his waist. I follow behind him, slow trying to let the one eyed monster calm down a bit.

As Dax enters the bedroom, he walks over to my little table and pours himself a Crown Royal. He returns to the bed, taking a sip on his way. He sits on the side of the bed, handing me the glass.

"What was that about? Why did you push me off of you?"

"Oh, it wasn't anything bad, I just wanted to come out here with you is all." I take a drink, place it on the nightstand, and open the drawer underneath.

I pull out condoms and KY jelly, setting them next to the glass. Dax scoots back, and props up on a pillow, I climb on and straddle his thighs. He throws his arms behind his head. I undo the towel, exposing his dick. With my hand, I begin stroking up and down his silky rod. It's already giving me a hard on again. The strokes are smooth and steady, Dax moves his hands to my towel, doing the same thing, and it drops behind my ass. His hand curves around my cock, and he starts moving up and down on me.

We both glide at the same speed on one another and our dicks smooth up against each other. I'm waiting for him to tell me which part he wants me to touch and how he wants to do this.

Dax flips me over on my back, and straddles me, like I was just doing to him. He grinds his dick against mine.

"I want to fuck you," he moans.

I just smile. Now I know where to go with this. I'm going to have to walk him through this though.

"Okay, get the rubber and gel Dax." He leans over grabbing it. He hands it to me, and I unwrap the foil packet, handing him the condom.

"Do I put it on now?"

"I do, if you're really ready to do this." I flip the rubber in my fingertips.

"Hell yes I am."

I slip the condom over the head of his dick and roll it down his shaft. He watches me, not saying a word.

"Now, you spread KY all over yourself and around my hole. It takes a lot, so lube up extra good. When men have sex, it's different than a woman. Men have muscles that have to be relaxed, you have to enter slow, okay? I'll walk you through it."

He squeezes out the lube on himself, and I help him spread it around on his dick. His expression is serious; he's really into this, almost like a Science project.

"Now, you have to do me, with the lube that is," I laugh.

He laughs, and pushes the gel into his hand, spreading it to his fingers. He raises his body off of my legs, and rubs his hands between my cheeks entering into my hole.

"Is that enough?" he asks, still fingering me.

"Yeah, you're good. Now get back in between my legs."

"God, I feel stupid Damien." He hangs his head down.

"Nothing to feel stupid about, it's your first time, and I don't mind telling you step by step. How else would you know?"

"Thanks. I guess all these instructions kind of kill the mood for you, huh?"

"Not mine, my mood is just fine. And by the looks of it, yours is fine too." I point a finger at his dick. He grins back.

"Guess it is then."

"Come hither." I wiggle a finger to him teasing him, and he leans over me. I give him a sloppy kiss. I take his bottom lip into my mouth, and lick my tongue against it. He tugs back on it, and I grab him behind his neck, jerking his mouth to me. We lap at each other, and I get even more wound up at his moans.

Dax backs away from the kiss, and lifts my legs, hooking them over his shoulders. I know he's about to enter me, and I start fondling myself.

"Go slow and easy. Remember, I have to be stretched slowly."

He nods and lifts my ass off the bed. I clench my legs holding on behind his neck. I feel the slight stretching, as he slides the head of his dick into my asshole. The look on his face is fucking amazing. He's a super tight fit for me and that radiates all over his face.

He slips back out. "Oops, sorry."

I smile and he enters again, pushing a little further this time, and slipping back, but not all the way out this time. He pushes in, I continue stroking myself. He's looking down, watching himself, as he speeds up a little.

"Ah, fuck Damien." He licks his lip, never moving his eyes off of himself entering me.

"Feel good?"

"Fuck yeah it does."

He pushes all the way inside me now and I moan. When he hears me moan, he power thrusts two quick jabs in me.

"Yeah, just like that Dax, you got this." *God he feels so good.*

"Mmm…"

I could almost get off right now looking at the concentration that covers his face. He bites his bottom lip, and I stretch my arm out to caress the side of his thigh, as he pushes in again.

With his hand, he grabs at my cock, so I let go, and he begins stroking me instead. His movements on my dick are in sync with his thrusts into my hole. I'm not going to be able to hold out. His rams into me speed up. His nuts slap against my ass and the sound is erotic as hell.

His juts into me faster and faster. I want him to enjoy all of this. I slap his hand off my cock and he slips them under my ass. I take over control of my own dick now, stroking hard and fast.

"Shit," he moans out, making me want to come all over myself.

"You got this. God you feel fucking good inside me."

He leans his head back and slams all his hip power into me. His last thrust sends shivers through my whole body, causing me to cum at the same time. His legs shake, like an earthquake hit. My thick jets of milky cream squirt all over his chest and stomach, as I feel warmness filling the condom covering his cock.

"Yesssss…fuck yeah." Dax yells out, and then relaxes, panting as hard as I am. He opens his eyes and stares at me. He slips out of me, and leans down to kiss me. His kiss is slow, and passionate.

"That...was incredible Damien." He tries to catch his breath.

"It was, wasn't it?"

"Oh yes." A childlike grin spreads across his face.

He rolls off to the side, taking a drink of the crown. Sticking his finger in it, he drips it over to my mouth, and I lick it off, sitting up.

"I think we need another shower."

"I think you are right Damien. Let's go!" He bounces off the bed, like a teenager. He's too funny. He tossed the condom in the trashcan.

Chapter Eleven

Dax is prepping our dinner for tonight. He's an excellent cook and definitely knows his way around in a kitchen. This entire last week of being with him has been a blast, but unfortunately, I'll have to go in to work tomorrow. The rain let up this morning, and it's time to get back to business.

I sneak up behind him, and wrap my arms around his waist.

"You know that I can't get anything done with you wrapped around me, right?" He stirs the noodles boiling inside the pot on the stove.

"I know, that's the whole plan. It's been a few days since our shower night, thought maybe we could break this three day dry spell."

"Hmmm…sounds good to me, but let me finish dinner first, it won't be that long."

"You could always just turn it off for a bit." I shrug my shoulders.

"Who likes a soggy noodle?" He wiggles both eyebrows, then burst out laughing.

I wrap my arms around his waist. "Come on, just for a few minutes?"

"Nope, step away from me with your evil seductive ways." He can't stop laughing, it's so playful. He crosses two fingers in a cross at me.

"You are wicked fine, you know that?" I slap him on the ass, then back up.

Dax snatches the kitchen towel that hangs on the oven door, and winds it in circles in the air.

"Don't do it, I mean it." I hold my hand out in front of me to stop him.

He gives me a wink. "Don't do what?" He snaps the towel at me, several times in a row.

"Stop, dammit."

"Getting angry Damien?" I grab the end of the towel and he tugs it back towards him.

No way in hell am I letting it go. When he jerks it towards him, he pulls me with him. I slam into his body and he lowers his head sucking my lip into his mouth, then pulls back making a smack sound.

"Oh, when you were upstairs, someone named Ron called for you. Said he was one of the foremen on the site, and needs you out there to check the soil levels tonight."

"Ah shit! I have to go. Apparently water must be standing instead of draining out. I need to see what's going on and determine if we need a dredger out there."

"Damien, how are you going to see anything? It's dark outside."

"We have homemade entrance ramps up to the sites every mile or so, I'll just drive up there and use my headlights. I've done it a million times."

"Can I ride with you?" He turns and faces me.

"No, just stay here, it won't take long. I should be back in an hour or so." I walk to the entryway and slip on my boots.

Dax walks up behind me and gives me a kiss. "Be careful."

"Well, it's not like I'm going on a covert mission or anything, I'm going to shove a stick in some mud. I think I'll be fine." I snatch my keys out of the basket and smile at him.

"Hurry back!" He straightens the collar on my shirt then gives me another kiss.

I slip the truck in reverse, and back out of the garage, making sure to hit the clicker to lock it back down. Thank goodness the site isn't too far. It'll take more time for me to do the tests than for me to get there.

I light a smoke, as I enter the ramp. Pulling directly in front of the first place to test, this place is a freaking mess. Without a doubt, I'll need a dredger, but I still need to double check for paperwork purposes.

My waders are in the toolbox in the bed of the truck, so I slip them on over my jeans and go to the area. I pull out my notepad to track everything. Geez, the men working here left in a hurry when the rain hit. They left wood and rebar all over the place. They never cleaned up the concrete rocks that are in clumps from the last concrete pour either. I jot it down in my notes, this is unacceptable.

Headlights appear, entering the ramp. It must be Ron coming to give me a hand, no one else knows I'm here besides Dax. He parks next to my truck leaving the lights on. His lights brighten the place up a little more, but it's still hard to see anything out here. There's not any side roads yet, therefore, no streetlights, no traffic or anything. I continue my evaluations.

The truck door slams, but I can't see him, the lights are blinding me. I look back to my stick, trying to get white spots out of my head from the headlights when I hear him nearing me.

"Hey Ron, this is one big clusterfuck dude. I'm glad you called. We're definitely going to have to get that pump down here to clear this water out, or we'll be on hold for another two weeks."

"I'm not Ron."

I'd recognize that voice anywhere. I jab the stick into the mud and turn towards him.

"Aaron, why are you here? What the hell is going on?" I cross my hands across my chest in defensive mode.

"I told you I needed to see you, too talk to you Damien."

"And I told you no. Wait, how did you know I was out here?" Instinctively, my hands drop to my hips.

Aaron reaches down, grabbing a two by four lying on the ground. His fingernail chips the wood splinters off of the end. One end of the board sticks into the mud on the ground, the other end, is what he's fidgeting nervously with.

"You didn't answer my question Aaron."

"I made the call to your house." He drops his head, almost looking shameful, and definitely guilty.

"Whoa, what did you just say? You called my house pretending to be Ron? Seriously?" I'm fucking pissed, how dare him.

What in the hell is going on with him? Who does he think he is? He's mad and upset, I already knew that, but to try to trick me to get me away from the house, away from Dax, is pushing things just a little too fucking far. That crosses stalker lines, I'll be damned if that happens.

"You need to leave Aaron." I pull my cell from my pocket.

"Damien, just let me explain, please. I love you, I really do."

"Dude, I think you need to get your head checked. Maybe you should have thought about that before you brought the hard dick into our bed. You don't even know what love is Aaron. Just leave before I call the cops."

I'm beyond pissed right now, I'm freakin' livid. How dare this bastard!

"Just tell me you don't love me, tell me Damien." He pleads with his hand out in front of him.

"I don't love you Aaron. I'm sorry, but I just don't." My arms drop to my side, my cell still in one hand.

"You're lying, I know better. I guess you think you're in love with that pool guy huh? Is that what this is all about?" He drops the two by four board and shoves me in the chest demanding an answer.

Instincts kick in overdrive. I stomp back towards him and wrap my fingers around his throat. His eyes bulge a bit, and there's no readable expression on his face.

"Have you lost your fucking mind Aaron? I'll pop your head off like a zit. You leave Dax out of this, he has nothing to do with any of it. You got that?" I loosen my grip so he can answer.

"Take your god dammed hands off me Damien." His arms slide up knocking my hand from around his neck.

"You need to leave now." I let go of his neck and push him in the chest. "You're trespassing, not to mention stalking." I push him backwards again and it knocks him to the ground. "Get the hell out of here now."

I turn away from him and stomp back towards where I was working. I begin to dial the numbers to home, just to let Dax know in case this dickfuck decides to show up there. I cannot believe he is trying to pull this. I push the first three digits when I'm slammed from behind. Aaron's push knocks my cell phone from my hand, sending it flying into the mud. I turn, swinging my fist into him. I nail him so hard, he almost falls down upon impact.

"Leave me the fuck alone Aaron. I mean it already. I don't want to hurt you, but I will."

Aaron jumps up and knocks me square in the jaw. He stuns me. I almost lose my balance, but not so much that I don't knock him down in a rebound punch. I turn to walk away again. I just want him to leave. I really don't want to resort to this, but I will. He's not giving me a choice in the matter.

A dull thud to the side of my head causes my ears to ring, and everything starts to blur. I realize that he just punched me, and I'm falling into the mud. My ears start ringing, little silver spots start zinging through my eyes and a hard, sharp pain blasts through me.

"Fuck you too Damien." I hear Aaron's voice through the searing pain in my head.

Everything goes dark.

Chapter Twelve

Dinner's almost done and ready for when Damien gets back. Tonight, it's Italian night. On the menu we have a fresh tossed salad, with Balsamic Vinegar to start with. We'll follow it with homemade beef and cheese manicotti. The manicotti is stuffed with ricotta and cottage cheese, onions, bell peppers, garlic, and ground beef. I smother it in a homemade sauce, topped with another layer of cheddar and Parmesan cheese, oregano and basil. Last but not least, garlic bread, it's browning in the oven now. The house smells amazingly like an upper scale Italian restaurant.

It's incredible here, I love it. If someone would have asked me a month ago, where I'd be now, this would not have been one of my answers. I'm glad things are working out the way they are.

Never in a million years, could I have dreamed I would be attracted to someone so quick, especially not to a man. I've always had an open mind about most things and situations. My relationship with Damien is a marvelous one, we get along terrific, and I find him surprisingly sexy. *Who knew!*

The dinner table is set, but he's still not home. Damien's been gone for several hours, I'm starting to get concerned. I pick up the phone to call him; it rings four times, and then goes to his voicemail. Damien usually always answers his phone, no matter who is calling. He's responsible for too many workers not too.

Another forty-five minutes has past and he's still not home. In conversations with him, I know exactly where the site is located. I'm going to the job, because something isn't sitting right. He would have answered, or called me if he was going to be this late. We'd never actually discussed what we would do if a situation like this ever came up, but I know he'd let me know something.

On the way to the job, I try to call him two more times, still nothing. Now I'm getting very worried. Once we get back to the house, we'll have to exchange important numbers, just so we have them. I drive past the makeshift ramp. *Shit!*

My truck jumps the curb, to get to the ramp. A wave of relief sweeps over me when I spot his truck. I pull up behind him and kill the motor. With my finger, I brush through my hair, and spray a squirt of cologne on me before getting out.

It's a real good thing I wore boots, everything is muddy. As I pass Damien's truck, I notice how dim his headlights are. He's damn near killed his battery. If his battery dies before he can get back with the keys, I'll give him a jump with my cables. Not smart on his behalf, he knows better than this.

I continue taking longer strides to search for him. He's nowhere to be seen. Off to the side of the work area, there is a small construction trailer, and two green port-a-potties, so I walk that direction.

The lock on the trailer is secure and it's dark inside. I holler out for Damien, but get no answer. I check the portables and they're both empty.

Shit, I have no idea where he could be? Maybe I didn't go far enough down the actual site, it's hard to see out here in the dark. I track back over, and walk a little further. The part of the road they are laying is a single lane that runs along the side of the freeway, where it would normally only be separated from the feeder road by a median, and it stretches about a two hundred feet.

I see the fresh footprints in the mud, so I follow them. Water is standing inside the new road. It looks to be about a foot deep. Straight ahead, I trace my line of vision, until I see something. I'm sure it's just materials for the job, but I walk another ten feet, and see it.

"Damien, Damien! Oh fuck me, shit!" In a panic, I run to him, my heart is about to beat out of my chest, I can't catch my breath.

Damien is lying on his back, near the dropdown. *Oh God!* Damien's body is half submerged in the muddy water, his clothes are drenched. He's not moving. *Fuck!* I grab him underneath his knees and behind his neck, raising him to the surface, and laying him flat on the muddy ground. I shred my shirt over my head and wad it up to place under his head.

"Damien, can you hear me? Damien!" I slap his face. *Please!*

Damien's stomach rises and falls, thank God, he's breathing. His pulse is thread, but it's there. I need help for him, quick. Dammit, my cell is back in my truck.

"Damien, I have to get my phone, to call for help. I'll be right back, I have to go to my truck."

I sprint to my truck, just as Damien's headlights die out. What the fuck happened to him? I slam my truck door open, and jump inside and start it. I snatch my cell, hit 9-1-1, and throw it in gear, pulling up closer to him. He's still lying there, not moving. I dig around my toolbox, jerking out a towel.

After my call goes through, I give the best description of where we are, and ask for an ambulance and police. I run back to Damien, still on the phone with the emergency operator. She informs me that the units have been dispatched.

With the towel, I go to cover his chest and arms, but stop. He's got blood all over him and his face is bruised. I reach around his head gently, until I find the source of the blood. His head is split open. I pull out my pocketknife and tear long strips off of the towel, and I wrap several layers around his head, tying it at his forehead. I lay the remainder of the towel down him long ways.

"Damien, can you hear me? Who did this, what happened?"

The sirens sounds are getting closer. I feel helpless. I'm not sure what to do now. I want to hold him close to me, but I know you're not supposed to move someone in case they're in internal damage. I already moved him from the water and lifted his head to wrap him.

"FUCCCCCCCCCCCCCCCCCCK!"

My pulse is racing, fear waves all through me. I'm fucking helpless right now, I can't do anything, it's out of my hands. My neck muscles tighten. My heart hammers in panic. Adrenaline surges, twisting into anger, then fear and frustration. The deep pounding of a bass drum vibrates in my ears, I think it's my heartbeat. Not again, please not again! Images of my brother play out in my mind, like an old movie. This can't be happening again. I should have been here. I could have stopped this, or I could have helped him. I never should have let him come alone. I wasn't here for him, just like I wasn't there for my own brother. How fucking stupid can I be? Pacing in circles, I run my fingers through my hair and squeeze the side of my head near my temples. *God Dammit, please help him...please!*

Red and blue lights highlight the night sky. I rush back to Damien, but trip and catch myself with my arms. I raise myself back up noticing the hunk of concrete that tripped me, lying behind me. It's covered in wet, glossy red blood all over it. That has to be what he busted his head open on, but it doesn't explain the bruise on his face. Someone must have hit him. There are two sets of fresh footprints here besides mine.

Think, think! I'm infuriated at the fucking bastard who did this. Damien is one of the nicest people I've ever known. Someone's ass is mine, guaranteed!

The police show up first. I flag them down, waving them over to Damien.

"He's here, right over here. He must have hit his head on the rock over there, it's bloody, and there are footprints."

"Are you the one who found him this way?" The officer pulls out his clipboard, while another officer checks on Damien.

"Yes, Sir."

"What is your relationship to the victim?"

"I'm his, uh…roommate." I break eye contact with the officer, looking towards Damien, then back to the officer again.

"What brought you out here, after dark, in a separate vehicle?" I put my hands on my hips, not really liking where he is taking this conversation at all.

He rattles off about ten thousand questions over the next few minutes. The paramedics pull up. They bring a gurney, loading Damien onto it.

"I'm going with him," I demand.

"Sir, we still have some questions and paperwork to fill out first, then you can take your own vehicle to the hospital. It should only take about ten minutes."

"Fine. I need a wrecker to tow his truck back to our house." I point towards his truck, but continue watching them carry him away on the stretcher.

I finish answering the questions, and I'm very much aware that I'm a suspect, their only suspect at this point, but I don't care. I just need to get to the hospital. I told the wrecker driver to just leave the keys in the floorboard of Damien's truck.

I'll find out who did this, there were only two people who knew where Damien was going. Ron and myself and I didn't do it, so that leaves this dude Ron.

He'll be seeing me real soon. *Real fucking soon!*

Chapter 13

Riverside General Hospital is only fifteen minutes from the site, so I haul ass to get there, to check on Damien. The parking is in the flat lot right in front of the entrance. I stomp my boots into the concrete to knock off the mud that covers them. With my hands ahead of me, I bust through the double doors to the front desk to find Damien. The nurse behind the counter informs me that he's having tests and scans done. It'll be at least two hours before he's assigned a room, he's still unconscious, but all of his vitals are stable at the moment.

I'm fucking livid pissed. I'm having a hard time calming down, and it's not these peoples fault. Whoever hurt Damien has a damn death wish. I'm going home to take care of business. This Ron and I are about to have a 'go to church' meeting, Texan style.

I toss my keys in the basket and walk to the phone. Scrolling through the call history, I get the number. I push star sixty-seven to block my number and call it back.

"Hello."

"Is Ron around?"

"Sorry, wrong number." The man hung up.

My ass wrong number, really? I start pacing the floor. It's the number that called our house, I know that's the number, I took the call. And that's his voice, it's familiar to me. I light a smoke and stare at the phone. This is bull-fucking-shit. I know that was his voice, the voice that called. Why would he say it wasn't? Our home number isn't showing up, it's coming from an unknown number. I write down the number.

After running upstairs to change out of the muddy clothes, my cell rings. It's the nurse from the hospital, Damien is awake and in a room. I grab the paper with Ron's number on it, shove it in my pocket and sprint downstairs.

The bike…I run out the garage door, and hop on my Hayabusa! And I haul ass to the hospital. I have to make sure he's going to be okay. I haven't been this scared since my brother.

The door to Damien's room is cracked, so I push it open a little further. On the left wall, it's full of shelves, a cabinet for hanging clothes, and a television rack up close to the ceiling. The bath is cadi-cornered between two walls, in the corner of the room. The other wall, on the right, is where Damien's hospital bed is located, with a chair, and nightstand near. There are a bunch of hospital buttons and intercoms systems located behind his bed, and down the other side of the wall. Against the furthest wall, it's taken up by a huge window with bench seats in the windowsill.

Damien is sound asleep, so I sit in the chair watching him. Attached to one arm, there are two IV lines, one with fluids and the other looks to be an antibiotic of some sort. On his other arm, there's a blood pressure cuff, and one of those finger pulse clips.

His hair is pulled to one side and there is a bald patch covered with a bandage that stretches around to the back of his head. You can see the imprint from the staples holding his head together! He looks bad, real bad. He busted his head far worse than I could tell in the dark.

Oh GOD, help him! I can't fight the silent tears! He's helpless. He needed me and I wasn't there for him. It's a repeat of my brother. This IS my fault. This happens to anyone I've ever been close too. I can't and won't let it happen to Damien, not after this. This is too close of a call. I should have been there.

Talk about having some fucked up karma. I take the cake, eat it, and hurl it back out for the next victim. I didn't mean to have feelings for Damien, they just happened, but it was too late to stop them. Now history is repeating itself. I got close to someone, now they're lying in a hospital bed. I have to go now. I have to get away from him for good.

I'll leave a 'Dear John,' letter on his hospital food tray, and then I'll walk out of his life for good. I'm thankful for what Damien has shown me, this path in my life, but I'm also sorry I ever met him. If I wouldn't have, he wouldn't be here in a hospital bed. I think I could even fall in love him, but I bring trouble. He doesn't deserve that.

Without him seeing me, or me waking him up, I scribble a note, leaving it on his tray table. It'll be there come next meal. I leave taking one last glance back at him.

On my way out, one of the nurses tells me that when Damien was awake, he told the police it was Aaron who attacked him. It's been filed now, they will handle it and arrest him.

My blood is boiling at the news about Aaron. I can't even think straight. Just let me run into him somewhere.

I hit the elevator button to take me down to ground level.

Still livid about Aaron and the whole situation, I stroll through the crosswalk to the parking area.

As I put my key in the ignition on my bike, I take a glance around the lot. The dickbag is walking towards the entrance door. I pull my key out and stomp towards him. I quick-scan the parking area and it's all clear except for us. *Perfect!* I dodge through the parked cars and walk up quietly behind him.

I reach out, and grab his shoulder, turning him to face me. When he sees me, his eyes bulge out, he knows what's coming. Aaron tries to break loose, but

I have a death grip on him. He's not going anywhere. This motherfucker hurt Damien!

"Dax, I fucked up. I love him, I didn't know. I'd never do anything to hurt him. It was a reflex, heat of the moment. We fought and I left. I didn't know he was hurt so bad."

I have no time for this shit I don't want to hear anything that he spews out of his mouth. I step up to him and swing with all my might. He drops straight to the ground. He moans and I kick him in the ribs.

"You hurt someone I care about!" I deliver another kick, knocking the wind from him. "I should fucking kill you, you know that?"

I kick repeatedly, making the last kick straight to his face. I snap and realize my anger has never been this bad, I stop. Blood pours from his head and face. He's still breathing and god damn lucky for that much. I turn and walk away.

I crank my bike and pull out of the parking lot. I have no particular place that I'm going. I just have to go away. Being with Damien was great, but I just can't do this. I can't believe that I allowed myself to have real feelings for someone, I know better than that. It was by accident, and I never meant too, but they crept up on me without me even realizing it.

What happened with Damien just brings back too many memories of my brother, and I can't go there, it hurts.

It's just time to disappear.

Chapter 14

The nurse barges through the door and half of her equipment crashes to the floor. Startled, I sit straight up in bed, trying to focus, and get a grip on exactly where the hell I am. The nurse apologizes and comes over to the bed. She immediately pushes the blood pressure machine and it begins to clamp around my upper arm. She places her hands on my eyelids lifting each one up and looks into my eyes.

"How are you feeling Mr. Davis? How is your eyesight?"

"I can see fine, but I have a monster headache though." I reach for my head.

The nurse yanks a little notebook from her shirt pocket and copies the numbers off the blood pressure machine. I scan the room looking for a sign of Dax.

"Do you remember what happened Mr. Davis?"

"It's Damien, no not really." I touch the bandage around my head.

"What is the last thing you remember?"

My head starts banging when I try to think. "I was at the site working. Wait, Aaron showed up, and we argued. That's the last thing I remember."

"One minute, let me get the police officer on your case to come take your statement. You seemed to have hit your head on a concrete rock, we had to staple the incision, and you have a concussion. I'll send the doctor in later to speak with you. Let me get the officer."

Police officer? She walks out the door and returns with a cop holding his clipboard. He passes me his card with a case number on it.

"Hello there, Mr. Davis. How are you feeling?" He looks out the window, ignoring me.

"Confused, and I've got a horrible headache. I'm starving too." I knew he didn't really give a flying fuck how I felt, but I gave him an answer anyway.

"So, tell me what you remember about tonight."

"I remember being at the site, and arguing with Aaron."

"Who is Aaron? Did you have an actual fight with him?" He jots down notes.

"A physical fight, sort of. We had an argument and there were a couple of punches thrown. He's my ex." I look back to him, to watch his expression.

"What exactly happened?"

I explain the whole situation to the officer, and all I get in return is an 'I see.'

"I'm still not sure why I'm in the hospital though. Where is Dax?" *I have to find him.*

"I'm not sure where Dax is, but we've already taken his statement. Dax is the one who found you and called for help. It appears that you were punched and fell hitting your head on a concrete rock."

"Wait, you're telling me you think Aaron left me there, unconscious and bleeding? And Dax found me?" I'm really confused now.

"It seems that way, yes."

"So, what happens to Aaron now? He just left me for dead? Amazing!" *What the fuck?*

"Well, we'll be filing charges on him for assault with bodily injury."

"What exactly does that mean? What will happen to him?"

"It's when a person assaults someone. They can be charged if they intentionally, knowingly, or recklessly cause bodily injury to someone else. What will happen to him depends on his past record. If he's had other assaults, then he could be facing prison time behind this, along with a hefty fine."

"Where is Dax?" I scoot up into a sitting position and my head starts throbbing.

"I'm not sure. I need to speak with him. At the time, we didn't have enough to hold him, but we thought it possible that he was involved."

"No, no way. Nurse, has anyone been here to see me?"

"Yes, tall, blonde man, tattoos, and a strange name. He was here earlier, but didn't say when he'd return. Let me get the doctor to come in, so you we can get you something to eat." She gives me a smile and walks out of the room with my file.

113

"Mr. Davis, one last question, do you have an address where Aaron can be located?"

"Yes, he'll probably be at his brothers or his parent's house. Or at the very least, they will know where he is staying."

"Okay, thank you very much. I'll be in touch." He walks out of the room.

I honestly cannot believe that Aaron just left me there, I could have died. How does someone just snap like that, he was there pleading his love, yet he didn't bother to get me help or anything? What kind of person does that? I guess no matter how well you think you know a person you never truly understand everything about them.

I need Dax. I want to see him, to thank him for putting two and two together, and coming for me. I could have died out there, Dax saved my life. God, how do you repay something like that?

The doctor enters, does his once over and okays me for release in the morning. He also gives the thumbs up for food, and gives me a shot for pain.

Now, if Dax would bring some of his manicotti, since I didn't get to make it for the dinner he prepared, everything would be great.

I close my eyes and doze off for a bit. The nurse returns with a food tray and moves the rolling table stand over my bed.

There's a note with my name on it. I recognize the writing, it's from Dax.

Chapter Fifteen

Unfolding the letter, I feel a bit uneasy about it. Why would Dax need to write me a letter, when he could just come here?

Damien, I'm so relieved that you are okay and that I was able to get to you in time. If I would have gone with you in the first place, this would have never happened to you. This is the kind of thing I explained to you, why I have a hard time being in any kind of relationship. I really care about you a lot, and it's also the reason I have to say goodbye to you. I don't want anything bad happening to you ever again, and when I'm around, that is certain to happen. It's the story of my life. It always happens to people I care about. I can feel myself falling hard for you, even though it hasn't been long, the fall is still hard. I wish nothing but the very best for you Damien, and I also would like to thank you for all you have given me, and shown me.

With Love ~ Dax

Fuck no! This is not happening. My heart just grounded out in my stomach. This isn't his fault. He doesn't have anything to do with what's happened, that's all on Aaron. There is no way I'm losing him. I reach for the phone and dial his cell number. It goes to voicemail. I call the house number, but it's the same. *Shit, how do I get a hold of him?* All my other numbers for him are at the house. I need to get home.

The nurse removes the tray of food and brings in a dose of pain meds. I get drowsy again. I can't keep my eyes open.

***

One of the nurses enters with a breakfast tray. Food doesn't even sound good, I can't think of anything but Dax, I even dreamed of him. Surely he doesn't really want this, for us to be apart, does he? I try his cell again, but still no answer. I send a text message.

Please don't do this Dax!

An hour later there is no return text. The doctor has come and gone, and now I'm just waiting for the nurse to unhook the IV's from my arm. The phone in the room rings, it's the cab downstairs waiting for me. The nurse hands me the paperwork and sends me on my way.

The cab pulls up outside my house. Dax's truck sits in the driveway and I'm really excited to see it. *Thank God!* I peel off forty bucks for the driver and get out.

I try to rush to the front door, but I'm still a little light headed, and have to slow my pace, or fall out in the yard. Granger greets me as I open the door. I toss my keys in the basket and holler out for Dax.

Not answering, I head up the stairs, and push his door open. Nothing! Only a small suitcase on his bed.

He has clothes packed in the smaller suitcase but his big one is gone, and some items are missing from the closet.

Back downstairs, I check the garage. His bike is gone. *Fuck!* Okay, okay…this means he has to come back to get his things at some point. Yes, he's not going to up and leave like this, not completely. What I have to do is convince him to stay when he comes for his things. How the hell do I do that when he thinks this is his fault?

In the kitchen I open the fridge and pull out some left overs to eat. The manicotti Dax made sits on the top shelf, so I fix a plate, nuke it, and sit at the table.

Why can't I even sit here without thinking about every conversation we ever had right in this spot? I know Dax thinks that somehow this is his fault, but it's not. He guilt trips himself about his brother, and runs from getting close to people, I just need to show him it's okay. Everything is safe with me. I'm not going anywhere and he doesn't have to be afraid. I yank out my cell and text him again.

I'll never let you down, don't be afraid. I hit the send button.

Fifteen minutes passes and nothing, again. Dammit! I put my dishes in the sink, kicking my feet up on the couch, and grab Dax's shirt that hangs over the end of it. I wad it up in my hands, bringing it to my nose. His smell is intoxicating, it reminds me of his kisses, and his gentle hand. For someone so manly, he's still so loving and tender. It brings back more memories. Nope, there is no way I'm letting him go this easy, not without a fight. I text again.

Please don't do this to us. Let me know you are okay! Send.

The phone beeps, and I press the icon for text. It's Dax.

I'm okay. I'm sorry Damien!

Can we talk? I send back.

I can't.

You don't have to do this Dax! Just come home. I miss you and I'm about to break. I just can't.

Come look into my eyes and tell me that.

You don't understand Damien! I'm not running from you, I'm running for you.

If you have to run, then run to me instead. I need you.

Ditto, but I can't. This hurts, you don't understand Damien.

YES I DO DAX!

He doesn't respond back. I know he's scared, but I am too. I'm scared of losing him before we ever get started.

I can't make him listen, when he can so easily turn his phone off, or not respond. I have to make him understand, make him listen to me, but I don't know how.

I don't feel right when he's gone. I feel broken and torn. We've been together such a short time, but I know him, I understand what he's going through. This isn't right! I need to see him, to show him.

My heart feels empty and stepped on. He refuses to back down out of fear that he'll hurt me, but he's hurting me now. I have to make him see this.

Nighttime comes, and I take Granger and head to bed. My thoughts are going crazy, missing him. He has to come back. We have to work this out.

Chapter Sixteen

A week has passed since my release from the hospital. In three days I have to return to get the staples removed from my head, and I'll get the all clear to go back to work. Besides headaches on occasions, there doesn't seem to be any kind of damage from the injury or the concussion.

Aaron was arrested, the day after my release from the hospital. He's tried to call me collect, several times from the Harris County jail, but I refuse to take the calls. He been set a bond, but no one will post that, not that I can think of. His brother and parents don't have the money. He'll be going to trial. One thing the cop did explain, is that because of his record, he'll be charged with his third assault offense. Apparently when Aaron was still in high school, he got into a fight with another student, and they were both charged as adults, even though he was only seventeen years old when it happened. The other time is when he was twenty-one, he was involved in some sort of bar fight and picked up his second assault charge. Now this is his third charge. Texas is strict on the third strike you're out rule.

The weather has continued to be off and on with storms, so no progress has taken place on the site, nothing has dried up enough to continue yet.

I haven't heard from Dax, although I do text him daily. I miss him terribly, but I have no clue where he is. I can't make him return my calls, but by texting every day at least he knows I'm still thinking about him. I give him an update, to reassure him that I am still okay. I hope by doing that, he'll understand that he's not causing me any problems. It's almost driving me to a breaking point not knowing if he's okay. Even if he just let me know that much I'd be a million times better.

Today, the rain has stopped and I'm going out to the site. No one is working, but I need to come to grips with what happened. Before taking a shower and getting ready, I send off a text to Dax.

Hope you are okay. I'm going to come to terms with what happened today, and go where it happened shortly. Just something I need to do. I miss you terribly Dax. Please let me know you are okay. Send!

After my shower, I dress and go out to my truck, heading towards the site. Dax never did text back, but I didn't expect he would. I pull up the ramp to the site.

There are ruts all over the dirt makeshift drive, it must have been from the police and ambulance when they were here. I walk out to where I was, but I can't see anything. Any blood has washed away from the site. The only thing I do notice is a flat indention in the mud, I have no idea what happened there or what it's from.

I bend down and touch the mud, closing my eyes. I'm trying to remember anything after the argument with Aaron. I'm not sure why this is important to me, but it is. His footsteps, I heard him come up behind me. We pushed each other and threw a couple of punches, I told him to leave, and pulled out my cell to call home. I remember a thud to my head, but it didn't seem hard enough to knock me out. I don't remember anything after that, except hearing him yell 'fuck you' at me.

My measuring stick, the one I used to test the samples, is still stuck in the mud where I left it. My feet are heavier than normal, but I stomp down through the mud to get it, and then turn to go back to my truck.

When I turn, there he is. *Fuck, my heart drops to the pit of my stomach.*

His blue eyes pierce into mine, I freeze. I'm not sure how to react or what I'm supposed to do. I don't know what to even say. A sea of emotions tidal wave through my body. My heart races and my pulse increases. I can't even take a step, I feel like I'm stuck in quicksand. My head tingles. *Oh God!*

"Are you alright Damien? You look like you've seen a ghost."

"I-um…yes. I'm okay. I wasn't expecting to see you." *I want to run!*

"Are you disappointed?" He stares into my eyes.

"No! Um…god no."

123

Come on feet, move now. I strain lifting one of my boots from the quicksand, I mean mud. One foot comes loose, then the other. I take a step towards him, then another.

A foot in front of him, I reach out, touching his cheek. The stubble on his face pricks into my fingertips, it's rough. I lean up pressing my lips to his.

"Fuck I missed you so much Dax," I whisper.

"I've missed you too."

I slide my cheek and it brushes up against his. I give him caresses with my face next to his. My body gets warm, and my heart beats fast again. Instinctively, my hands wrap around him, and he wraps tight around me, giving me pecks on the forehead.

Dax pulls me tighter and I fall into a comfort zone with him. Holding each other, not a word is said. It doesn't need to be. His head rests on my shoulder and I bury mine into his chest.

This is where we belong, this is safe and secure. This is right.

He leans back, raising a hand to my neck, and grips behind my hairline in back. With his other hand, his fingers rest under my jaw, but his thumb is on my chin. He gives a slight pinch, as he tilts my head up. I dig into his back and clench him. He parts my lips with his tongue. Slowly, he licks into my mouth, his tongue flicks against mine igniting feral desire in me. His tongue slurps across my lips and he sucks my top lip into his mouth. I've never been kissed this way in my life. With his arms around my back, he raises his shoulders, kind of hunching over, and pulls me into him. His tongue licks, following with a gentle pucker, to my lips. Dax cups my cheeks in his hands as he pulls me into him. His thumbs deliver brush strokes, like a painter, to my cheeks. His eyelids, at half mast, are sultry and sexy. He closes his mouth over my lips, sucking me into his mouth, and then rests his lips at a standstill against mine.

Dax leans back and it takes everything I have to open my eyes. He reaches for my chest, and I take his hand, kissing inside his palm then hug it to my face.

I grab him tight, kissing him again, but he pulls away.

"How are you feeling Damien? Why are you here at the site, shouldn't you be resting?"

"I'm good, I feel all right. I go next week to get these staples out. I came here because I needed some closure, I guess. Hell, the man left me for dead. I needed to face this and get over it before I come back to work. How did you find me that night?"

"When you didn't come home, I remembered you telling me where your site was, and I had a feeling something was wrong. You would have called if you were going to be late. I just drove until I found you. You were lying over there halfway in the water. I drug you out of the drop down and laid you down somewhere around here. It scared the living shit out of me. I had to run to my truck to get my phone to call for help, and then I wrapped a towel around your head. You were bleeding a lot, but you weren't moving and your breathing was staggered"

"That's what that is, where you drug me out and laid me down?" I pointed to the flat part of the ground. "I wondered. Thank you, thank you for saving me Dax."

"Saving you? If I would have been here this wouldn't have happened." His shakes his head side to side. "If I never would have come into your life this wouldn't have happened in the first place Damien."

"If you wouldn't have come for me, I would be laying here, probably dead Dax."

He turns and walks back toward his truck. I follow him.

"Let's go home," I smile.

Dax climbs on his bike and kick starts it. "I can't Damien. I'm sorry."

Chapter Seventeen

What the fuck just happened? Dax turns a half circle and races off down the ramp. I'm confused. I understand he had to sort out thoughts, but how does he show up now only to turn away again? It doesn't make sense. None of this computes, I thought we were both going to get through this together, at least it's how I imagined it.

With my hands in my pockets, I look around like I just lost my best friend. Dammit! I fish the keys out of my pocket and get in my truck. I'm not even sure how to wrap my head around this. All I can do at this point is head for home. A million thoughts run through my head, but I can't process any of them yet. I'm not sure how to handle it, or which direction to send the thoughts. This is too overwhelming to grasp.

My cell phone rings as I pull into my garage at home. I click the green button to answer and put the phone to my ear. "Yup?"

"I can't do this Damien."

"Fuck!" I take a deep breath. "Dax, think about this before you decide to give up on us. Are you worried what people will say about us being together? Or is it your fears about losing someone, this self-imposed curse you put on yourself, about things never working with people you get close to?" Dax lets out a little laugh, yet I want to lose it and damn near break down behind it.

What's so fucking funny about this? I slam the gear into park and turn the key to kill the motor. I drop the phone in my lap and palm slap the steering wheel with both hands. *Fuck!* My heart plummets like a plum seed into the pit my stomach. I hear his voice yelling my name and pick the phone back up.

"You're misunderstanding me Damien."

"No, I'm not. You've explained it all to me, I understand every single word, I get where you're coming from, but dammit we fucking work together. We work as a couple and you know it. You can't just fuck it all off like this. You're killing yourself with denial and you're taking me with you. It's not fair to either of us Dax."

"Quit talking." He gets quiet over the phone, so I wait. "Look in the rearview mirror already."

"What?"

My eyes shift to the rearview mirror. Dax is sitting right behind me on his bike. His heel catches the kickstand, and then he raises his long leg over the seat, dismounting.

I smile from ear to ear, looking like a kid amped up on Halloween candy…goofy grin and all.

Overwhelmed and grateful, my head drops to my hands in relief. I take a deep, cleansing breath, and Dax opens the door.

"When I said I can't do this, I mean be without you. I'm not denying this anymore."

I search his ocean eyes to see if he is serious, if he really means this. With the back of my hand, my knuckles stroke his cheek, and I close my eyes. *Yes!*

In a matter of a few words, 'look in the mirror,' and seeing the sincerity playing out in his eyes, he means every word of it. Men don't get butterflies in their stomach, but I've got what feels like a full blown ostrich kicking and flapping around in there. I can hear my heartbeat thumping in my eardrums. No more smoke and mirrors going on here, everything that was distorted just became clear.

I twist my finger into the neckline of his T-shirt, gripping tight, and step out of the truck. I lead him behind me, not saying a single word. We enter the back door and he kicks it closed with his boot. I spin around to him pushing him in the chest, and slam him against the wall. I spread his legs apart, delving forcefully between his lips with my tongue. The tension builds and the anxiety excites me. I refuse to let this feeling go, he wants me, and I want him. This is the masculinity, self-confidence and self-assurance in yourself and your partner. It makes me feel like a man. I lick between his moist lips, winding my tongue around his, swallowing the groan that rumbles from his chest. Still holding tight to his neckline, I slip my other hand behind his neck, pulling him tight against me. The hairs on my body stand on edge. He grabs my jaw, holding me tight, and guides my head to match his return assault on my mouth. Our mouths widen, thrusting hard against one another.

Dax lets out another gasp. God he makes me shitfuck horny. I run my hands under his shirt, shredding it from his skin. I push against him, grabbing his ass in my palms, and squeeze him hard.

Dax pushes back against me, slamming me into the opposite wall. He snakes his body down mine, and winds back up me, grinding into me like an 80's rock star on a mic pole. *Oh fuck this is hot!*

His dick is hard as steel crushing against me. I grab his cock through his jeans, and rub up and down the thickness. He lets out a monstrous moan and I swallow him.

He quickly moves his hands to his crotch and unzips his jeans. I grab the waistband, fighting him, to rip them from his body. His hands force over mine, grab the sides, and yank them down over his hips. Jeans down to his knees, he kicks off his boots, sending them flinging across the laundry room. He pushes his pants to the floor with his feet. If he only knew how fuckable he looks doing this. I dart my tongue across my lips in a lick of pure want and need, savoring the sight of him. There's not a single inch of him that I don't want to taste. I grab him by the hair and jerk him to my mouth, slurping his wet and hungry mouth in mine.

He presses against me, and I slide my knee between his legs, rubbing against his rod. I have to get him balanced, and bent the hell over something now. Stagger-walking him towards the kitchen counter, I slam him backwards into it, sending the loose mail scattering to the floor tiles.

His hands grope and grab at me, and he yanks me out of my jeans like a damn pro.

He gives me an eat-you-up grin, and squats down in front of me, taking my cock into his mouth. His wet warmth engulfs me, hard and quick. I grab his shoulders, as he tightens his lips, puckering back and forth over the head of my prick. He lets out a garbled moan, my dick aches with his touch and sounds. I almost get off listening to him.

"Fuck you feel good, but stop Dax."

I push his head off of me, staring down at his lusty dick. "My turn."

I kneel in front of him, flicking his balls with my tongue, as my hand wraps around his hardness. I lick down his gooch, inching towards his hole. He spreads his legs apart, allowing my head to squeeze between them. I reach my destination, and swirl my tongue around the rim of his ass, as he lets out a deep and throaty moan. Driving my rigid tongue inside of him, I give quick, hard flicks gyrating in and out of him. His moans are driving me insane. *I fucking love it!*

Dax bends a bit, pressing himself into my face. I slurp at his rim again, making sure it's nice and wet

131

so I can insert my finger. I remove my mouth and slip a finger inside him, making circles in his depth, stretching him before I add another. I insert the second finger, with a skin tight fit. As I push into him, my mouth goes back to the cock at hand, literally.

I purse my lips over the head of his dick, taking him part ways in my mouth before slipping back to the tip. He pushes a little further into my mouth, and my saliva moistens his cock, making him downright slippery. I curl my tongue around his shaft, while working my fingers into his manhole. The vein that runs down the underside of his dick is swollen, and I trace it with my tongue, before taking him a little deeper in my mouth.

His hands wrap up in my hair, and he pulls me to him, thrusting his body into my mouth. I'm going to have him this time, all of him. I continue prepping him with my fingers, and I know it won't take much, and he'll be spewing his juices inside my mouth. I need a condom and some lube.

Still on my knees, I move my available hand, reaching for my jeans that he shredded off of me. My wallet's inside my pocket. I'm always prepared, so I pull out the condom. Now for lubrication, it's upstairs, but I have some baby oil in the medicine cabinet in the kitchen. That is going to have to work for now.

I slide my mouth from around his cock and stand back up. My lips touch his and his tongue slams into mine. I pucker him between mine and mumble.

"I need lube." I plunge into his mouth again. "You're mine, I'm taking you this time." He grasps behind my head, yanking me into him.

I'm surprised we didn't chip our teeth with his forceful yank. I back step towards the cabinet and swing my hand up to open it. His kisses don't let up, and all I can do is fumble with my hand, until I recognize the bottle. Finally I grab it. I hand him the condom and he pulls back, placing the foil wrap in his teeth and ripping it open. He pulls the rubber out of the package.

"Put it on me." I instruct him.

Dax looks down, placing it at the tip of my cock, rolling it with two fingers down my cock, leaving the tip loose. Once he has it on, I swing him around, facing him towards the cabinet and countertop.

"Give me that ass of yours, I'll be easy. Just remember that you have to relax though, okay?" He nods.

I wrap my arm around his chest, leaning into him, smelling his manly scent, and licking his back. I push against his back, and forcefully bend him over the counter, making him available to me.

I kick his legs apart, grabbing the oil from the countertop. I squirt a little drip in his crack, letting it trickle down and then I work it into him with my fingers. I coat the condom on me, sliding my hand up and down my own cock, and then dangle myself between his ass cheeks.

I've dreamt of this moment, taking his virgin ass, but I know that I have to go slow and gentle. I have to be very easy with him since it's his first time receiving.

The very tip of my slick dick presses into him, as I guide myself with my hand, my other hand on his ass cheek pulling him apart. Pressing through the skintight hole, my legs begin to shake at how narrow and small he is. I'd love nothing better than to slam myself into him, ramming every inch of my dick inside of him, but he's in no way prepared for anything like that yet.

I wrap my left arm around his waist. Taking a deep breath, I slip in through the ring of muscles that are tensing up. I pull back slow and gentle on him, hearing his gasp as I do. *So seductive.*

"Oh god Damien," he moans.

I slip back out all the way and then enter him again, pushing a bit further. His muscles tense, and clamp around my cock. I continue entering him deeper and deeper.

I look down, watching myself, as I slip in and disappear inside of him. I pull back a little quicker and speed up a bit more when I go in this time. I fucking love the sight of this, of him giving himself to me like this. How the hell do I control myself? The tight fit of his ass is incredible, and as it begins to contract, I almost lose all control. Taking my hand from his waist, I reach up his back, yanking his long ass hair. I can't wait for the day that I can wrap up in his hair and control him by the yanks given to him.

I reach around to the front of him, wrapping my hand around his cock, and start pulling him from the base to tip. I hold off on cumming, even though I want with everything inside of me, to spew inside of him right now. My mind is a one track spitting time bomb that needs to blow its load.

"I'm gonna come Damien," he groans between quick breaths.

I slam harder into him, until I feel his insides begin to relax a bit. Faster and harder, I slide in and out of him, until he takes all of me deep inside of him. He lets out a loud gasp. He's ready now. My nuts tense tight, and my body shakes from the top of my head down to my curling toes.

I slap my body against him. "Holy shitfucks."

My emotions twist all up in my head. I thrust faster and faster, slipping in and out, harder and harder.

"Oh god, I'm gonna come now," he yells.

Dax's legs quiver. I can't hold out any longer. I toss my head back, as I plunge into him. He pushes back against me, and I feel him tense, then spasm through his entire body.

"Shit...shit," he yells.

"Oh yeah, fuck yesss..."

My nuts tighten into balls of goddamned steel, and I slam quick thrusts into him. His warm sticky gel explodes in my hands, and his ass quakes in quivers against my cock. Tingles erupt goose bumps all over my body.

"Oh God," I breathe out, almost hissing.

The waves of ecstasy explode euphoria that sends sensations waving through my body and down my spine. I jab my last thrust into him, pounding deep and hard. His hole grabs me, and I spew elations of release inside his chamber.

Sweet merciful fuck!

My legs shake in delirium tantrum, and I get lightheaded and have to hold his hips to keep myself steadied.

I collapse over him, crumbling across his sweaty back. He fights to hold me up. I press my hands on the counter top and balance my weight on my hands instead of completely on him. My limp dick slips from his clenches. He rises back up and I stand.

"Oh my God, you were a fucking beast, so incredible!"

"You weren't so damn bad yourself." I laugh. "Fucking amazing, actually."

He turns to face me and I kiss him. "Let's go upstairs, where you belong...in my bed."

He gives me that saucy sweet grin and we both walk naked upstairs and crawl into our bed.

Chapter Eighteen

I thread my fingers through the hair that trails down Dax's back. He's beautiful when he's sleeping. All night long, we snuggled up next to one another, it was comforting and so secure. This is the way things are meant to be. I knew one day I would find someone who made me feel this way. There never was anything carved in stone during my relationship with my ex-wife, or even Aaron. Dax is the one for me, I just didn't know it. You know what they say about everything happening for a reason; well that's how it is with Dax and I. We had to both travel our own separate paths to get to this place and this very moment right now.

I haven't heard anything else from Aaron, I definitely don't miss him. I still wonder what causes a person to snap the way he did. The last I'd heard, he was still in jail awaiting his trial. I hope they give him the max penalty. I know he'd been set a bond, but so far no one has posted it for him. I kind of doubt if anyone will. His mom and brother don't really have that kind of money. Plus from everything Aaron had ever told me, his mother hardly talked to him anymore and his brother was just weird about him. He'd always assumed it was because he was gay.

Dax is spread eagle out on his stomach, his head faces away from me, and his hair trickles down his sexy back. He's got one leg cocked up, bent at the knee. I stroke down the length of his hair over and over. *He's got to be the sexiest man on earth.* The man literally reeks of adhesive pheromones, he's highly fucking addictive.

I trace from his hairline, down across his perfectly smooth and tanned back towards his ass. I grab him in my palm, giving a gentle squeeze. His skin is soft as silk. With his leg spread the way they are, it's like an open invitation, it's one I can't resist.

With two fingers, I outline his balls, massaging the soft skin with my hands. He tightens slightly, and I reach up under him until I have his cock in my hand. I rub against him and he lets out a deep moan, pulling his leg up tighter to his chest.

His cock starts to lengthen and becomes hard in my grip. My hand curls around him, I slowly work my way up and down his shaft. He lets out another moan, but doesn't move. He doesn't need too. I have easy access to him right now. I slide down on the sheets and lower my head, giving him a kiss on his left ass cheek.

My body sparks electrical charges all over me, it's like being attached to invisible jumper cables. I break out in goose pimples and my dick gets harder, just like his. I straddle myself over him, but never stop stroking him. With one hand, I support my weight as lean over and lower myself against to him.

My cock twitches in pleasure, as I slowly graze it across his ass. I situate my body so that my hanging dick can slide up the length of his crack and slip back down, but not entering. I jerk him a little faster and he moans again, moving his head slightly.

I kiss his neck then twirl my tongue in tiny orbs of passion against his skin. I know he loves this, and somehow the nerve receptors in his neck have a direct connection to his cock. It's an instant stimulator.

"Mmm…yes." He moans, then yawns.

"Good morning hotness. Does this feel good?" I ask him, still slurping his neck.

"Uh-huh, it feels great." He scoots his body around on the sheet and presses himself down into me, gyrating and grinding his cock against my hand.

I continue licking and deliver kisses to his earlobe and temple. I nibbling and flick my tongue across him. "Turn over for me delicious," I whisper in his ear.

I lift up and he flips over on his back. I hover over him, as he gets comfortable. Lowering myself to him, our dicks touch first, and I start air pumping against him. I let our dicks collide, bumping and poking into one another.

He puts both of his arms behind his head, fingers locked together and he tilts up to watch me. The feel of his hard dick against mine is wicked hot. I take our shafts, cupping us together in my hands and I continue to wiggle back and forward with him just a little. It's like jacking off two rods at the same time almost, it feels awesome.

"You feel so fucking good Damien."

"Mmm…it does feel good, doesn't it? I want to feel you inside me again Dax."

He immediately stretches his long arm over to the drawer next to the bed, pulling out a condom and the gel, then he rips the package open. The lube drops on the bed. He looks down at his dick and slips the rubber on the head, rolling it down his shaft. Next he takes some of the gel and squirts it into his palm and lubes himself up real good, the way I showed him. I love watching him skate up and down himself. It makes me hornier than I already am. He's just so fuckable. I lick my lips with my tongue, he looks up and busts me watching him. He bites the inside of his lip, never losing eye contact with him. I gaze from his eyes and that seductive fuck me look he's wearing, to his mouth. It's sexy the way he bites inside. I shift my gaze back down to his hand sliding up and down his monstrous cock.

As he pours some of the lube on his fingers I lift up slightly. He slips them into me, slow and gentle, in and out, then he twists his fingers from side to side. I love how he makes his fingers like scissors, and spreads me a little bit at a time. He presses deeper into me, his wrists twists sideways and pulls out of me almost to the tip, then shoves back in, straightening his fingers again. Once I loosen up a bit, I lean over him, squatting down onto his cock. I take him inside of me and guide how fast, and deep he enters me now. I love this position, feeling him deep into me, real deep, is hot as hell.

I raise myself and lower again, over and over as he delves deeper into me. Once his cock squeezes past my inside muscles, I take him all the way, as I sit down on him. *Fuck, fuck, shit!*

"Oh fuck yeah."

Dax closes his eyes, moving his hands from behind his head and greedily grabs my cock. He tugs on me, yanking my cock towards him. He takes the gel and squirts a little on my hard dick, then swipes up and down my length.

"Oh yes, just like that Dax, deeper."

He thrusts up into me. "You like this?" He slams into me again.

"Fuck yeah I do. I love the way you feel inside of me, it's so good. I love riding you like a brahma bull."

I let out a loud moan as he pumps into me again, with more force. I bounce up and down on him, and he jacks my dick harder and harder.

"You're so tight."

I slide back down on him and my nuts tense. *Sweet merciful fuck.*

"I'm about to cum already." Dax pushes into me.

"Do it Damien. Cum all over me."

With those words, he works me faster. His quick jabs into me cause my body to tense, and we both release at the same time. He lets out an incredibly hot moan and the warmth inside me is unbelievable. My juices squirt and jet a stream on his stomach.

"Oh fuck yeah…" I can't control my breathing, I'm practically gasping for air now. I relax down on him, pressing my body against his.

"Holy hell Damien, what a way to get woke up. Damn!"

"You like?" I give him a shit-eating grin.

"I more than like it. Feel free to do it whenever you like."

I slide off of him and sit on the bed beside him. The expression on his face gets serious quick. He stares deep into my eyes. *I knew it, I fucking knew it!* I've tried to work this out in my head, but didn't want to bring it all on him at one time, at least not until he was ready. Now he is. I rotate towards him, and stroke my hand across his cheek. For a few minutes neither of us say a word, somehow our eyes just already know how this is all going to work out.

"Dax, people can say what they want about love and love at first sight, about how falling for someone takes more time, blah, blah, blah." I cup his face in my hands and give him a smile. "But my reality is crystal fucking clear. No ifs, ands, or buts. Loving someone isn't about what you can live with or accept and tolerate. For me, it's about the one person you can't live without. Too know that your life will never be the same without that one person being a part of it."

He sits up and leans back against the headboard. He flashes a grin and reaches out to me. I lean over towards him and take him in my hands again. His fingertips brush against my bottom lip.

"Are you saying you love me Damien? That I am that one person for you?"

"Is that..." I suck his lip, "what you want me to say?" I bury my tongue in his mouth again.

"Mmm...hmm." He pulls out of my mouth. "Yes, but only if you mean it."

"I do mean it, I love you Dax. You are the man I can't live without." I squeeze his face and lean closer to kiss him again. It's slow and gentle this time, romantic and passionate. He runs his hands through my hair, I lean back.

"I know it's strange, but what you said about people thinking it's too soon to fall in love or that people don't know each other, I used to think like that...until now. You changed all of that. I somehow went and got all passionate and you became my perfect passion. I love you Damien."

He pulls me into him, brushing his lips against mine, gently parting with his tongue. I could do this all damn day, I swear.

"A perfect passion huh? I can live with that."

143

I lay against him and his arm wraps around my shoulder pulling me in tight to him. I caress his stomach then put my head against his chest. A perfect passion, this is what we have. I don't plan on ever letting this go.

The End

Epilogue:

I've been watching them for days now. I can't believe he could just move on like that. I see them laughing and playing around together, having their own little private moments of touching and teasing. He never did that before, it makes me sick.

I can tell you one thing, this shit is going to end, that is a fact. Maybe what I did was wrong, but there was no emotional attachment to the hard dick I brought home, he was just a good fuck is all. There was no heart involved, no emotions, just rampant tantric sex. I'm not sure why he doesn't get that.

The whole situation makes me crazy in the head. Night after night I camp in my car, parked outside, with a perfect view of the bedroom window.

Tonight, I'm going past that. I need to hear what is going on with the two of them. They both act like love struck puppies. He is mine and I will have him back. I know once he sees me, he'll take me back. Everything was just a huge mistake, I can explain it to him.

***

It's been dark for a couple of hours and I know their routine like clockwork. They go upstairs and watch TV and god knows what else, before falling asleep. I should be able to get in. Granger won't bark, he knows me, so it should be good. I'd had a copy of his house key made a long time ago.

I check to make sure none of the neighbors are outside and step out of the car. I approach the front door, sliding my key into the keyhole, turning it. Click! The lock opens. I turn the knob and let myself in, closing the door slowly behind me.

I search for Granger, but he's nowhere around. *For fucks sake, does he still let that damned dog sleep with him?*

Making sure not to make a single peep, I tiptoe towards the stairway. The first step creaks. The footsteps of Granger get louder and he lets out a large bark. Fuck!

"Shhh Granger, come here boy, come on." I whisper quietly and the mutt comes to me.

"Granger shut up boy." The shout comes from upstairs.

"Good boy, good boy. Go lay down now." The dog pounces back upstairs after I pet him.

I take quiet steps until I reach the top floor. I hear them talking, but I need to be closer to make out the conversation. I tiptoe closer, now I can hear, in fact I can actually see them through the crack in the doorway.

"I just don't see how they could release him, what the fuck is going to keep him from coming here? He could be anywhere at any time really."

146

"I know Damien, I know. Surely Aaron's not stupid enough to do anything, not with his court date pending."

"Sure he is Dax. The man's an unstable, psychotic fuck, he tried to kill me."

My blood is boiling. Did he really just call me a psychotic fuck? He acts like I'm crazy or something.